WHEN A CALL GIRL CALLS

Call him Ralph.

Better yet, don't call him. At least not before noon, because if you do he's liable to answer on about the eighth ring and say something like:

"Whoever you are, you'd better hang up right now, or I'll find out where you park your car and do something in the gas tank you won't like."

The caller on this occasion paused. "I don't own a car. Is this Ralph?" The voice belonged to a woman.

"Who the hell is this?" said Ralph.

"This is Lyla."

"Who the hell is Lyla?"

"Lyla Dane. I live in the apartment above you. We see each other every day."

"The hooker."

"You live over a dirty bookstore. What do you expect for a neighbor, a frigging rocket scientist? Look, I'll give you a hundred bucks to come up here now."

"Ain't it supposed to be the other way around?"

"Jesus Christ. You coming up or not? I got a dead priest in my bed."

Bantam Crime Line Books offer the finest in classic and modern American mysteries.
Ask your bookseller for the books you have missed.

Peeper

Loren D. Estleman

BANTAM BOOKS

NEW YORK · TORONTO · LONDON · SYDNEY · AUCKLAND

PEEPER

A Bantam Book
Bantam hardcover edition / November 1989
Bantam paperback edition / October 1990

Book design by Anne Ling.

ISBN 0-553-28605-6

Published simultaneously in the United States and Canada

Bantam Books are published by Bantam Books, a division of
Bantam Doubleday Dell Publishing Group, Inc. Its trademark,
consisting of the words "Bantam Books" and the portrayal of a
rooster, is Registered in U.S. Patent and Trademark Office and in
other countries. Marca Registrada. Bantam Books, 666 Fifth Avenue,
New York, New York 10103.

PRINTED IN THE UNITED STATES OF AMERICA

OPM   0 9 8 7 6 5 4 3 2 1

To Rob Kantner
in memory of *Stones in the Sky, Mad Dog*,
and other stillborns in the age of awakening.

Chapter 1

*C*all him Ralph.

Better yet, don't call him. At least not before noon, because if you do he's liable to answer on about the eighth ring and say something like:

"Whoever you are, you'd better hang up right now, or I'll find out where you park your car and do something in the gas tank you won't like."

The caller on this occasion paused. "I don't own a car."

"Then I'll do it to you."

"Is this Ralph?"

The voice belonged to a woman. He could tell, because on mornings like this anything higher than a male tenor set his hangover on edge. "Who the hell is this?"

"This is Lyla."

"Who the hell is Lyla?"

"Lyla Dane. I live in the apartment above you, for chrissake. We see each other every day."

"The hooker."

"You live over a dirty bookstore. What do you expect for a neighbor, a frigging rocket scientist?"

Ralph Poteet sat up in bed and rumpled his mouse-colored hair. His head felt like grout. He fumbled the alarm clock off the night table and held it very close to his good eye. He laid it face down and whined into the receiver, "It's two-thirty ayem!"

"Hey, thanks. My watch stopped and I knew if I called you you'd tell me what time it is. Listen, you're like a cop, right?"

"Not at two-thirty ayem."

"I'll give you a hundred bucks to come up here now."

He blew his nose on the sheet. "Ain't that supposed to work the other way around?"

"Jesus Christ. You coming up or not? You ain't the only dick in town. I just called you because you're handy."

"What's the squeal?"

"I got a dead priest in my bed."

When she had repeated the statement, he said he was on his way and hung up. He sat there for a minute moving his tongue around inside his mouth. It reminded him of an armpit. When he moved, a square gin bottle slid off the blanket. He caught it before it hit the floor, saw it was empty, and dropped it. He shambled into the bathroom, which had started out as a closet and seemed determined to stay that way, and emptied his swollen bladder into the toilet with his forehead resting against the slope of the ceiling. While thus engaged he went through his morning catechism, asking himself his name, his address, and where he had spent the evening. He got the first right, wasn't sure about the second, and drew a blank on the third. He was doing better than usual.

Back in the bedroom he put on his Tyrolean hat with an orange feather in the band and after a brief search found his suitpants on the floor half under the bed. These he pulled on over his pajamas. He stuck bare feet into his loafers and because it was October he tugged on his suitcoat, grunting with the effort. He was forty-three years old and forty pounds overweight. He looked for his gun just because it was 2:40 A.M. in Detroit, but it was a halfhearted attempt; he hadn't seen it in weeks. He gave up and went out. The hallway smelled of condoms and cooked cabbage.

Lyla Dane's buzzer was the only one in the building that worked, not counting the one on the ground floor that the landlord used during police raids in election years. The door snapped open. Lyla was just five feet and ninety pounds in a red kimono and pink satin slippers with white butterflies on the toes. She wore her black hair very short.

"You look like shit," she said.

"That's what two hours' sleep will do for you. Where's the hundred?"

"Don't you want to see the stiff first?"

"What do I look like, a pervert?"

"Yeah." Stepping away from the door she drew a key from the pocket of the kimono and unlocked a drawer in the lamp table. Inside was a metal box, from which she took a brick of paper currency and counted a hundred dollars in twenties and tens into Ralph's palm. She put the rest back in the box.

"I thought broads always kept their valuables in the bedroom." He counted the money again and pocketed it.

"That's why I keep mine here."

She locked the drawer and led him through a small living room decorated by K mart into a smaller bedroom containing a Queen Anne bed that had cost twice as much as all the other furniture combined and took up most of the space in the room. The rest of the space was taken up by Monsignor John Breame, pastor of St. Balthazar downtown, a cathedral Ralph sometimes used to exchange pictures for money in his favorite pew, although not so much lately because the divorce business was on the slide; no-fault was killing his livelihood. He recognized the monsignor's pontifical belly holding up the flesh-colored satin sheet. The monsignor's face was purple.

Ralph found a Blue Diamond matchstick in his suitcoat and stuck the end between his teeth. He was beginning to feel better already. "He a regular?"

"That's the kind of question I don't answer. Tonight I thought he was breathing a little hard after. Then he wasn't."

"Well, he's deader'n Pope John."

"Thanks again. I thought he was imitating a fucking Buick."

"At least he wasn't a fag." He rubbed his bad eye. "I guess you wouldn't know where I was last night."

She hesitated. "It sure wasn't here."

"It'll come back. So what do you want me to do?"

"Get rid of him, what else? Cops find him here the Christers'll run me out on a cross. I just got nicely established."

"Cost you another hundred."

"I just gave you a hundred."

"That was for coming up. You're lucky I don't charge by the pound. Look at that gut."

"*You* look at it. He liked the missionary position."

"That fits. What's a hundred? You don't even take 'em all the way off for that."

"Son of a bitch."

"Yeah, yeah."

She left the room and came back with the second hundred. This time he didn't bother to count it. "Take a walk," he said. "Come back at dawn."

"Where'll I go?"

"There's beds all over town. You probably been in half of them. Or go find an all-night movie if you don't feel like working. What am I, a cruise director? Use your head for something besides head."

"Funny. That's new since Coolidge." She started to untie the kimono, stopped. "You going to watch?"

"What's the matter, you work with the lights off?"

"You didn't pay to find out. Move it or lose it."

He moved it. She slammed the bedroom door. In the living room, still chewing on the matchstick, he wandered over to the lamp table and tried the drawer. It was locked. He picked at the mechanism with the matchstick. Lyla, in white panties and a peach-colored bra, came out of the bedroom carrying the key, opened the drawer, and took the metal box with her into the bedroom. He admired the English in her tight backside.

Five minutes later she emerged wearing a canary jumpsuit, tan jacket and a red wig that needed an aircraft light. She had on working makeup; her lashes were longer and twice as thick, her face less round and not as puffy under the eyes. Something about the way she handled her brown shoulderbag told Ralph he would find the metal box empty.

"So it's work."

"I got to make back two hundred by sunup." She paused at the door to the hallway. "What are you going to do with him?"

"You really want to know?"

"I guess not. Hell, no."

"Good hunting."

"Go fuck yourself."

When she had gone, he helped himself to a can of Budweiser from the refrigerator in the kitchenette. He helped himself to another and then he went back into the bedroom and looked up a number in the metropolitan directory. He sat down on the edge of the bed and used the pink telephone on the night table. He was feeling better by the minute.

While he was waiting for someone to answer, he patted the monsignor's sheet-covered foot. "What do you say, Father? She worth it?"

"Yes."

He swallowed his matchstick. When he finished coughing it up, he realized someone was on the line. He cleared his throat. "Is this Bishop Steelcase?"

"It's three ayem," said Bishop Steelcase.

○○○○○○

"Thank you. My name is Ralph Poteet. I'm a private detective. I'm sorry to have to inform you Monsignor Breame is dead."

"Mary mother of God!" The harshness went out of the bishop's voice like air. "What happened?"

"I'm no expert. It looks like a coronary."

"Mary mother of God. In bed?"

"Yeah."

"Was he—do you know if he was in a state of grace?"

Ralph produced another matchstick. "See, that's what I called to talk to you about," he said.

Chapter 2

*H*e had time to kill. When he was through talking with the bishop, he worked the plunger and dialed the number of the adult bookstore downstairs. It rang a long time before a voice like ground glass answered.

"Jesus Christ. Hello."

"Vinnie, this is Ralph."

"It's three-thirty ayem!"

"Thanks. Listen, I'm up here at Lyla's."

"Oh yeah?" There was a leer in his voice; but then there was generally.

"I need my camera."

Pause. "Who you going to get to take the pictures?"

"Cut the crap. Can you bring it up?"

"You going to pay me the rent you owe?"

"I just want to borrow it."

"Last time you borrowed something from me I had to buy it back from a fence."

"It got stolen from my car. We been through that."

"What was you doing with a five-year run of *Screw* magazine in your car?"

"You going to let me have the camera or not?"

"You got six hundred bucks?"

"Hell, Vinnie, it ain't worth fifty. The shutter sticks and the flash don't work."

"When you left it here you said you paid two hundred for it."

"Listen, if I give you fifty can I have it for an hour?"

"Cash?"

"No, I thought I'd put it on the Gold Card. Jesus."

" 'Cause that last check you wrote bounced from here to Lansing."

"Vinnie."

"I'll bring it up. You better have fifty in your hand."

Ralph broke the connection. Talking to Vinnie was like playing handball in a fish tank. Absently he pocketed a sterling silver ashtray he found on the night table.

Vinnie sounded like a professional wrestler and looked like the house eunuch. He had a round, perfectly bald head, round eyes, a round nose, mouth, and body, and when he walked he always stuck the sole of his foot out at an angle like a character in a comic strip. A childhood illness had claimed all his hair; Ralph had a bet with the bookie on his floor that Vinnie's crotch was hairless as well, but so far neither had had the opportunity to collect, nor wanted to. He stood in the hallway wearing a fuzzy yellow robe and dangling the camera, an old black Canon, from its strap at his side. "Where's the fifty?"

Ralph separated two twenties and a ten from his roll and laid them in the landlord's fat palm.

"That's some choke," Vinnie said. "If you went and hit the lottery, remember you're into me for six yards."

"Just give me the camera."

He gave it to him. "Where's Lyla?"

"Working late."

"Thought she worked at home."

"Not this morning." Ralph tested the focus. "You didn't see me go out last night, did you?"

"Seen you go out, heard you come in. About one o'clock, it was. That hat don't go with your pajamas."

"Anybody come back with me?"

"Sure, Cybill Shepherd and that Winger dame. The one in *An Officer and a Gentleman*. I guess you forgot."

"Go to bed, Vinnie. I'll get this back to you later."

"Maybe I better come in and look around. It ain't like Lyla to be out this time of the morning. She could get raped."

Ralph blocked the door. "That'd come under theft of services." He held up another ten. "Night-night, Vinnie."

"Happy photography." Vinnie took it and left.

"Don't forget to credit me," Ralph called after him.

He opened the back of the camera. Half the roll of film was exposed. After some thought he remembered it contained shots of Mrs. Wayne County Supervisor Horace Powell and a supermarket stock clerk named Hashmi. He had had plans for the pictures, but then Powell had been forced to resign over a kickback scheme involving sanitation-removal contracts and Ralph had not bothered to develop the roll. He deplored the escalating corruption in local government.

In the bedroom he turned on both lamps and adjusted the shades so that their light shone full upon Monsignor Breame's congested countenance. The fat priest looked as if he were scowling in the confessional. Opening the closet, Ralph flipped through the negligees hanging there until he came to one he especially liked, a see-through tangerine number with lace on the bodice, and arranged it at the foot of the bed along with a matching pair of panties he found in Lyla's dresser with WELCOME ABOARD U.S.S. JOYTRAIL embroidered in red above the crotch. Then he stepped back to survey the scene. It looked too contrived. He picked up the panties and hung them on the bedpost. "Perfect."

He took a dozen pictures from different angles, finishing the roll with an artsy shot from the foot of the bed that made the monsignor look like a corpulent Frankenstein, then put the roll in his pocket and went back downstairs to stash the camera in his apartment. Vinnie could sue him for it. Ralph had been ducking process servers since he was twenty.

Back at Lyla's he put away the negligee and panties and straightened the lampshades. Just then the door buzzer sounded.

"Poteet?"

The man was tall and gaunt, with a complexion like damp pulp and hair of no identifiable color, cropped down almost to stubble. His feet were large in black oxfords and he had big hands with scrubbed nails like a mortician's. He had on a black coat buttoned to the neck. His eyes had no whites and Ralph thought he looked like an early martyr.

"Yeah. You're from Steelcase?"

"I'm Carpenter."

That was the name the bishop had given him. He stepped aside and the man went straight into the bedroom without looking around. Once there he took in the scene.

"Lots of light."

"You ever been in a dark room with a stiff?" Ralph asked.

"A time or two. Is there a back stairs?"

"Just a fire escape. It ain't been used in thirty years. I wouldn't try to carry a grudge down it."

Carpenter studied the corpse. "He's bigger than I thought."

"You bring a hand truck?"

"No." He lifted the monsignor's bare arm from the bedspread and let it drop. "Help me dress him while he still bends."

"Who said we have to dress him?"

"Trust me. You don't want to carry a naked body down two flights of stairs."

"You talk like you done it before. What was it you said you do for the bishop?"

"I didn't say. The figure was a hundred dollars." Carpenter produced two fifties from a flat wallet. Cold fingers touched Ralph's as the bills changed hands.

"Well, what the hell."

The monsignor's clothes consisted of an ordinary gray suit cut for an extraordinary figure, a white dress shirt, and striped boxer shorts draped over a chair. He wore only a rosary around his huge neck. Carpenter got the corpse's right arm into a shirt sleeve and, grunting, lifted the upper body by the shoulders for Ralph to manage the other. The monsignor groaned.

Ralph leaped back, colliding with a wall. "He ain't dead!"

"Air trapped in the lungs. They always do that. Put his shirt on."

"You put it on. We'll split the hundred."

"You want to hold him up?"

Ralph edged forward and picked up the other sleeve.

The job took half an hour, long enough for Ralph to trade his loathing for exhaustion. The trousers were the hardest: Ralph, the only one of the pair with the necessary bulk, had to push the massive body onto its side and brace his shoulder against it while Carpenter finished tugging them on. They tied the monsignor's shoelaces and helped him into his suitcoat.

Ralph plopped into the chair and got out his handkerchief. "I wish Ma was here. She wanted me to get closer to the Church."

"Head or feet?"

He looked at Carpenter, who still had his coat on, buttoned all the way up. "Don't you stop to sweat?"

"I'm not paid to. It'll be getting light in an hour."

"Yeah, yeah."

Ralph took the feet. They knocked over a lamp and a cheap portable color TV, got the body into the hallway, and dragged its heels across the runner onto the staircase landing, where they stood it against the wall. Just then an old woman in a white babushka and black leather jacket came up the stairs carrying a purse the size of a valise.

Ralph, propping up the monsignor with a hand under his arm, smiled. "Good morning, Mrs. Gelatto. How was work?"

She stopped two steps down from the landing, reached into her purse, and put on a pair of tilted glasses with rhinestones on the frames. She peered through the thick lenses.

"Oh, it's you. Who's that with you?"

"Just a couple of friends. They're on their way home."

"You shouldn't let the fat one drive. He can't hardly stand up."

"We won't, Mrs. Gelatto."

"He looks dead. You boys should eat when you drink. It ain't healthy on an empty stomach."

Ralph made a sickly smile. "Well, good night, Mrs. Gelatto."

"Mr. Gelatto, he ate pickles. He said the dill absorbed all the intoxicants. The undertaker didn't even have to embalm him."

"We'll remember that. Good night, Mrs. Gelatto."

"He was a drinking man, but he was faithful."

"I'm sure he was. Good night."

"He didn't have no choice. Who'd sleep with a man smells like the kosher plate?"

"Ha-ha. Well, good night."

"Just be sure he don't drive."

"We'll call a cab."

"Better call a truck. Hee-hee." She put away her glasses, mounted the landing, and let herself through a door down the hall.

"Mrs. Gelatto," Ralph told Carpenter. "She cleans two floors of the Penobscot Building nights."

"Think she suspects anything?"

"She can't see to the end of her mop."

"Okay, give me a hand. We've got to turn him to get him down the stairs."

○○○○○○

"Can't we just roll him down? I got a medical problem."

"Better a hernia than postmortem bruises."

Once again, Ralph wondered what Carpenter did for the bishop. He was beginning not to enjoy his company.

The monsignor was getting stiff. Ralph put a headlock on him from behind—saying, "Excuse me, Father"—and, bearing most of the weight, backed down a step and then another while Carpenter held up the feet to keep from snagging the heels on what was left of the staircase runner. They stopped every few steps to rest. Ralph's nose was in the monsignor's collar most of the time, long enough for him to develop a lasting distaste for Old Spice.

Coming off the second-floor landing, his foot slipped. He felt himself toppling, tried to slow the descent by hitting the wall, managed to squash himself between the wall and his burden, said, "Woof!" and let go his grip.

"Catch him!" Carpenter barked. Ralph caught him.

Executing a graceful pirouette, the monsignor tipped forward down the stairwell with Ralph embracing him from behind. Ralph landed on top and tobogganed down the steps and through the narrow linoleum foyer, coming to rest with a crash against the heavy steel fire door that led to the street.

Carpenter joined them at the bottom. "Nice catch."

Ralph, sprawled atop the corpse, said, "I think I got a postmortem bruise."

Chapter 3

*T*he car parked in the loading zone in front of the adult bookstore was a midnight-blue Buick station wagon, full size. It looked black under the streetlight, and Ralph thought at first it was a hearse. He stood in the open doorway while Carpenter checked the street. Monsignor Breame lay on his face at Ralph's feet with his suitcoat rucked up under his arms. Ralph thought of a *National Geographic* special he had seen once when *Gilligan's Island* was preempted, about whales that beached themselves. He wondered with a grunt where he'd put his truss.

"Clear." Carpenter looked gaunter than ever and scarcely more alive than the monsignor under the forty-watt bulb in the foyer. "We'll put him in the front seat on the passenger's side."

"Why not in back?"

"It'd look like I was carrying a corpse. Besides, I need to see out the back window."

Ralph thought it would be more fun to put him behind the wheel, but said nothing. The door on the passenger's side was open. They cradle-carried him across the sidewalk—Ralph waddling now and sucking in his breath with each step—sat him on

○○○○○○
15

the seat, got his feet inside, and poked and shoved and pulled him by his lapels into an upright position facing the windshield. Carpenter adjusted the dead man's clothing and buckled the shoulder harness, straining it to its limits.

"Peaceful, ain't he?" Ralph's voice sounded a trifle high to his own ears.

"Watch him while I go up and make sure we didn't forget anything."

"Where in hell would he go? Sorry, Father."

"Just watch him." Carpenter went inside.

The street was chilly. Ralph closed the monsignor's door and went around and climbed into the driver's seat, drawing that door shut. After a minute he cranked down the window to let out the Old Spice. Just then a police officer came around the corner testing doorknobs.

Ralph said shit and slid down in the seat. The officer came over and shone a flashlight in his face.

"Something I can help you with, sir?"

Ralph sat up. "No sir, Officer, sir. I'm just waiting for my friend. He forgot his coat. Sir."

The officer directed his flashlight past Ralph, who shifted his position to prevent the shaft from falling on the monsignor's face. "Sir, is your other friend asleep or passed out?"

"He's hypoglycemic. I warned him not to have that second slice of lemon meringue."

"Looks like it was the whole pie."

The flashlight's angle changed. Ralph leaned forward, then sat back when the officer moved it that way. The beam shifted forward again, then darted back. Ralph was caught leaning in the wrong direction while the light settled on the monsignor's mauve profile. It rested there a long time.

"Does your friend need medical help, sir? He doesn't look so good."

"No sir, Officer, sir. A few hours' sleep and he'll be fine.

That's why we're taking him home, my other friend and me. Sir."

"Sir, are you making fun of the way I talk?"

"No, sir. I mean no."

The officer sucked a cheek. He was in his twenties, with a clean jaw and a sandy moustache and flat pale eyes under the squared visor of his cap.

"Wake him up," he said.

"Oh, you don't want me to do that." He bit back another *sir*.

"I said wake him up. If you can. Your friend looks dead to me."

"Dead?" Ralph arranged his face into a grin he knew was tortured. "Dead, that's a ripe one. Ha-ha, dead."

"Let's hear him laugh."

"He don't have much of a sense of humor."

"Or any other kind." The officer retreated a step and rested a hand on his revolver. "Get out of the car."

Ralph had a bad idea. What the hell, he thought.

He slid an arm behind the monsignor's back, saying, "Look alive, Johnny! How you feeling now?" He pushed the corpse's top half toward the dash. It groaned.

The officer relaxed. He took his hand off the gun.

"Sorry, sir. We can't be too careful in this neighborhood. It's hip-deep in weirdos. No offense, sir."

"Yes sir. I mean no sir. I mean no." Ralph had to grip the monsignor's coat to keep his head off the dash. "I guess you can't be too careful with all the weirdos in this neighborhood."

"That's just the way we look at it. Listen, you better get your friend home as soon as your other friend shows. He doesn't sound much better than he looks."

"Yes sir."

"It's four-thirty ayem, you know."

"Thanks, Officer."

○○○○○○

The officer continued down the block, rattling doorknobs as he went. Ralph let go of the monsignor and bit down on a fresh matchstick. Carpenter emerged from the building while he was spitting out the pieces.

"Jesus, what took you so long? A cop was here." Ralph got out of the car.

"I saw. He smell anything?"

"Naw, I handled him. I got to tell you, I ain't spent this much time with the clergy since Sister Mary Immaculata."

"You were raised Catholic?"

"My old man was a Baptist minister, you kidding? My wife tried converting me. It didn't take."

"Where is she?"

"Iowa or Idaho, or maybe it was Illinois. One of them *I* states."

"Divorced?"

"Got to be, by now."

Carpenter climbed in behind the wheel. "I'll take him from here."

"What you going to do with him?"

"What do you care?"

"Mister, I've known people twenty years I never kept this much company with at a stretch."

"Well, it's over now." He slammed the door.

"Listen, I'll keep my mouth shut."

Carpenter had started the engine. "What?"

"I said I won't say anything."

"Oh. Good." He rolled up the window.

Ralph stood on the sidewalk until the station wagon glided around the corner out of sight. He wondered if he should have waved; at Monsignor Breame, not at Carpenter.

He had two hours before it was time to get ready for work, but he wasn't sleepy enough to go back to bed. He shut himself in his tiny bathroom with the camera, took some developing solution out of the medicine cabinet, and turned off the electric bulb, opening the camera by feel. After twenty minutes he hung up the film to dry and let himself out of the bathroom. Two beers later he went back in, turned on the bulb, and examined the negatives against the light. Ralph thought the monsignor would have been pleased to learn how photogenic he was in death. Even the embroidery on the panties had come through. He took a minute to admire the shots of Mrs. Supervisor Powell and her Pakistani-American friend at the beginning of the roll, then consigned it to an aluminum mailer and hid the thimble-size container behind a broken section of the medicine cabinet that lifted out of the back. It was better than a safe because it didn't call attention to itself. In the past, Ralph had concealed everything there from a complete run of phony Rolex watches to a bag of marijuana that had turned out to be Nabisco shredded wheat.

Yawning now, he went back to bed feeling uncommonly well for 6:00 A.M. His hangover had lifted—even if he still couldn't remember where he'd been the night before—he had two hundred and forty dollars in his pocket, and photographs of a dead Catholic priest in a prostitute's bed. Things were looking up all around.

He woke up when a big black fireman chopped down his bedroom door with an axe.

"Where's the fire?" inquired the black man.

Ralph sat up and rumpled his hair. "Ain't that my line?"

"Wrong floor, Tyrell," someone called from the hallway. "Some broad's apartment upstairs."

"Sorry about the door." Tyrell withdrew.

Ralph said shit and looked for his hat.

Chapter 4

*T*he arson investigator's name was O'Leary.

His suit was smoke-colored and he had runny eyes that he kept wiping with a sooty handkerchief that left smudges. He was nearly as big as the fireman who had awakened Ralph and a couple of years Ralph's junior, with more smudges in his yellow hair and a big scorched-looking face with a small upturned nose that someone had tried to alter with a pair of pliers, leaving the end squinched and slightly twisted. He wrapped a smoky paw around Ralph's hand in greeting and ushered him out of the charred hallway into an empty apartment two doors down from Lyla Dane's. There he lit a cigarette and dropped the match at his feet. The carpet began to smolder.

"Too much smoke out there." He puffed up a great cloud.

Ralph said, "Smells like a wienie roast."

"That'd be the tenant. Know her well, did you?"

"To say hello to on the stairs. She going to make it?"

"By now she's on her way to the University of Michigan Burn Center in Ann Arbor, if she survived the trip to Detroit General. They do some nifty things there. What's she do for a living?"

"Hook. What happened, gas?"

"Probably. She entertain any visitors recently?"

"That's how she paid for the gas."

"Get a good look at any of them?"

"You don't look at johns if you can help it. One of them could be the mayor."

"Ever hear any loud arguments from her apartment?"

"There any other kind?" Ralph groped his pockets for a matchstick, then decided against it, given the company. "You saying the fire wasn't an accident?"

O'Leary wiped his eyes. "Just routine. You're not much help, Mr. Poteet."

"You should be asking Vinnie this stuff. He's the landlord."

"I tried. He wasn't any more help than you. What do you do?"

"Private dick."

"Really? With an agency, or are you a loner like Sam Spade?" He tapped some live ash onto the carpet. There was a little flame burning there now.

"Fuck Sam Spade. I work for Lovechild Confidential Inquiries on Michigan. I got to be there in a half hour." He had spent the past ninety minutes in the hallway with the other residents, watching the firefighters put out the blaze and the ambulance crew carry a blanket-wrapped Lyla Dane downstairs. Vinnie had found her crumpled at the base of the wall opposite her apartment door, where the blast had hurled her when she'd come home. Ralph had slept right through the explosion and the sirens afterward. "Listen, if some cookie is running around blowing up people in this building, I got a right to know it."

"We've got no reason to think anything of the kind. Fire resulting in casualty is our beat, that's all. Does this Dane woman smoke?"

"She does now."

O'Leary wiped his eyes, dropped the cigarette butt on top of its ashes, and put away his notebook. "Okay, I guess that's it. You got a number where you can be reached during the day?"

Ralph sorted through the cards in his grubby wallet and gave him one engraved on rose-colored stock with a flower in one corner. The arson investigator raised his eyebrows. "A dame runs the joint," Ralph said.

"Thanks for answering my questions, Mr. Poteet." O'Leary opened the door for him.

Ralph left after stamping out the fire in the carpet.

Vinnie was standing at the end of the hall by the stairs. With his hands in the pockets of his fuzzy robe and the light gleaming on his bald head he looked like Henry in the comic strips, except he had a mouth.

Boy, had he.

"What was you moving downstairs this morning, a load of bowling balls?" he asked.

Ralph had been expecting the question. "I tripped. You ought to replace that runner. It's been there since FDR."

"You ain't bruised. Something must of broke your fall."

"My hat. I got to go to work, Vinnie."

"I didn't tell the cop about you being in Lyla's apartment this morning."

"Why not? I got no secrets from cops." A truck shuddered by on the street outside. Ralph jumped. He'd thought it was thunder.

"Where's the camera?"

He made an embarrassed expression. "Damnedest thing. It was in my car—"

"Hell of a mess." Vinnie was looking at the damaged hallway. "My insurance won't cover it. I been meaning to kick it up, but the premiums are killing me now. The adult trade's gone to shit. You seen the stuff them video stores carry? I can't compete. There should be a law. Any kid can walk right in and rent a movie I couldn't show my wife."

ooooooo

"You married a stag queen, Vinnie. The first time you saw her she was under three guys and a husky."

"It was a malamute. That stuff's strictly PG next to them new videos. The business has gone to shit, all right. I guess peepholing's up."

Here it comes, Ralph thought.

"Yes, that was some noise you made this morning, you and your skinny friend," the landlord continued. His voice was low. "I thought it was them neighborhood vigilantes come back with an army tank. I got a good view of the foyer through my transom. Well, it was as big as a army tank, and there you was sitting on top of it. I hope I never get that fat."

"Spit it out, Vinnie."

"I ain't stupid. I guess I can put together a snooper and a camera and a whore and a dead guy on the stairs. I guess the cops could too. They tie it in with that big bang down the hall, there's trouble coming."

"The guy said it was a gas leak."

"That's how it could stay. If you follow me."

"Vinnie, I was lost when you started."

"You got till tonight to find your way back. That's about as long as I can expect the cops to buy that I forgot all about this morning. Half your action, that's all I want. What's half? You know where to find me when you make up your mind. Hell, I'm always here."

"I'm late for work, Vinnie."

He stepped out of the way. "I don't guess that matters if they throw you in the can."

On his way downstairs, Ralph stopped at his apartment, took the roll of film out of its hiding place behind the medicine cabinet, and dropped it into his pocket. He didn't trust Vinnie and his passkey.

*　　*　　*

The car he drove to work was a brand-new red Riviera convertible with white upholstery and a white top. It belonged to a lawyer friend who had asked Ralph to sell it for him while he was serving two years in Jackson for suborning to commit perjury, only Ralph hadn't gotten around to it yet. The morning was overcast and the wide streets had that granite look they took on just before a rain. As he navigated his way around the abandoned cars and construction barricades, he thought about the explosion in Lyla Dane's apartment. The building had had gas leaks before, but he kept coming back to Carpenter and how he had refused to explain what he did for Bishop Steelcase, and that last trip upstairs without Ralph. *Coincidence, that's the dick's best friend,* old Gus Lovechild had said once. *When your client's husband and his secretary check into the same motel ten minutes apart, that bonus is as good as in your pocket.* Except for that time with Judge Morganthaler and a file clerk from the Frank Murphy Hall of Justice, that is; which *had* been a coincidence. It had taken six months and a thousand dollars in an envelope addressed to a state police commander to get back Gus's investigator's license. But the rule was sound.

Still chewing over it, Ralph parked in a handicapped zone near the building on Michigan Avenue and spent a moment looking through the printed placards he kept in the glove compartment before selecting one that read VISITING PRIEST, which he thought appropriate. He clipped it to the sun visor so it could be read through the windshield and went inside.

The gilt lettering on the glass doors to the floor where he worked read LOVECHILD CONFIDENTIAL INQUIRIES. Beyond them the reception room was painted in rose and lavender on alternating walls with Lautrec prints hung on them in glass frames. The marble coffee table by the chairs and sofa supported current issues of *Vogue*, *GQ*, and *Architectural Digest*, and hidden stereo speakers piped Bach and Mozart into the room. It was impressive, but Ralph missed the old mustard-colored office with EAGLE

EYE DETECTIVE AGENCY flaking off the window and geriatric copies of *National Geographic*, the African issues, on the yellow library table. Behind the kidney-shaped desk sat a receptionist with hair like a cloud of platinum powder and daggerlike nails painted fiery red.

" 'Morning, Anita," Ralph said. "I guess you got to be real careful when you use toilet paper. You could bleed to death."

She didn't look up from her copy of *Working Woman*. "Mrs. Lovechild wants to see you."

"What's she want this time, my body?"

"Just your testicles. She said to send in that asshole as soon as he decides to show up."

"How'd you know she meant me?"

"A business is like a pair of pants. It can only have one asshole in it at a time." She turned the page.

He leaned over the desk and lowered his voice to a gruff whisper. "I hear the Alamo Hotel on East Jefferson is running a lunchtime special: fifty minutes for five bucks."

She looked up from her magazine for the first time, smiled, and aimed one of her nails at his good eye. "How'd you like to hustle pencils for the rest of your life?"

"Broads. Never a straight answer." He shrugged and went through the door behind the desk.

In the short pastel hallway that led to Lucille Lovechild's office, Ralph's personality underwent a change. He straightened his necktie, took off his hat, and smoothed back his hair, which flopped forward again as soon as he took away his hand. Holding the hat, he tapped softly on the door with the occupant's name on it engraved in a brass plate. He remembered the matchstick he was chewing and put it in a pocket.

"Come in, Poteet."

The office was twice as large as the reception room and decorated much less gaily, with a gray-and-white carpet, woodgrain paneling, and framed community-service citations on the walls.

Windows on the north and east sides looked out on Washington Boulevard and Woodward Avenue. The only thing feminine in sight—and that included Lucille Lovechild herself—was a spray of daisies in a cut-glass vase-on the gray steel desk. They looked as if they'd rather be anywhere else. Ralph sympathized.

"You wanted to see me, Mrs. L.?"

"You're late. As usual."

"There was a fire in my building."

"I thought maybe your sister was sick again. Have you got a sister, Poteet?"

"She's in the Ohio Hospital for the Criminally Insane. Her and my old man had an argument with an electric knife. It was a hell of a Thanksgiving."

The owner of the agency was standing at the north window gazing down at the street. She was taller than Ralph and lean, in her late thirties, with her hair up and frosted. She wore glasses with neutral frames and a tailored tan suit over a white silk blouse with a jabot at her throat. Her profile was clean and she wore very little makeup. Finally she turned from the window and placed spread fingertips on her desk.

"Do you want to tell me about this morning?"

"What, the fire?"

"Before that."

Ralph suddenly had to go to the bathroom. He wondered how many others had been watching him that he hadn't known about.

"This morning?" he repeated.

"This morning, last night, whichever you want to call it. When decent people are in bed. I want to know what you thought you were accomplishing."

"Who'd you talk to, the bishop?"

"What bishop? I'm curious to know why you thought it necessary to jeopardize your job by calling me at ten minutes past midnight and asking me about my sleeping habits."

"Huh?"

She took off her glasses. She had clear gray eyes and a level stare that reminded Ralph of her late husband. "Amnesia? That's your defense? Okay, I'll play. I don't appreciate being awakened in the middle of the night and asked if I sleep with a G.I. Joe doll."

"I did that?"

"You said you had a bet with a guy in the bar."

"Did I say which bar?"

"What difference does it make? What you do on your own time isn't my concern, thank Christ, but when it involves me I'll put on the iron boot and kick your lard butt from here to Kalamazoo."

"I was drunk."

"I wouldn't recognize you sober. And that's another thing. From now on there will be no drinking on company time."

"I meet a lot of clients in bars. They'll take it wrong if I don't drink with them."

"I'm talking about the fifth in the wastebasket by your desk and the pint in your glove compartment and the flask in your coat. You're a walking Seven-Eleven. Any clients you drink lunch with are not clients of this firm. I've made that clear.

"Lovechild is an inquiry agency," she went on. "That means we run credit checks, investigate employee theft, and look for missing persons. We don't handle divorce work. We don't peek through keyholes. Most particularly we don't sneak around taking photographs of consenting adults submitting to their biological urges, regardless of whom they happen to be married to."

"Yes, ma'am."

"When my husband died and left me the agency, his will stipulated that you would remain employed here for as long as you wanted. It didn't say in what capacity. That's why you work in the file room, shuffling records and drawing your salary. I won't have you out front where prospective clients can see you or talk with you or know you exist. You seem to think your job is secure no matter what you do. It isn't. You just haven't made enough of an ass of yourself yet to cause me to put my lawyer to work breaking the will. Last night's escapade came damn close. Am I clear *now*?"

"Yes, ma'am."

"You say, 'Yes, ma'am,' but you're really thinking, 'hard-nosed bitch,' aren't you?"

"No, ma'am."

"Then you're even dumber than I thought, because that's just what I am." She leaned forward. "I'm your worst nightmare come true, Poteet—a woman in charge, who's on your case. Every time you come into this office I'll have a new rule for you. Sooner or later you'll break one, and then you're history. I don't know what Gus ever saw in you, but I'll see the last of you yet."

"Yes, ma'am. Ma'am?"

"What?"

Ralph put on his hat. "You didn't say if I won the bet."

"Get out!"

He got out, fishing for the matchstick.

Chapter 5

*I*n the corridor that led to the file room he ran into Chuck Waverly. The young operative was in a hurry and almost dropped the file folder he was carrying.

"You sign that out?" Ralph asked.

"Yes—er—no. I'll do that when I put it back. I think I found a link to the Henderson thefts."

"You still working on that Klugman thing?"

Chuck raised eyebrows eminently designed for raising. He was in his twenties and very slender, with red hair and a face that Ralph always resisted the urge to pinch. "How'd you know I was on it at all?"

"I read the file. You're wasting time with the Dombrowski kid. Klugman's your man."

"You're supposed to file them, not read them. They're confidential."

"I read all the files. How else can I kill time back there, jerk off into the wastebasket? I read yours. You ought to marry that girl."

He flushed. "What makes it your business? Wait a minute. Becky's not in my personnel record."

"If all Beckys was, we'd be canned more often than strained peas. Didn't Lucille teach you nothing about getting more dope than you hand out?" He was grinning.

Chuck changed the subject. "So what's this about Klugman? He owns the place, why would he steal his own stock? We caught young Dombrowski ripping off Henderson's Department Store five years ago, and here he is again working for Klugman."

"We didn't catch him, *I* did. It was just before Gus kicked off and Our Lady of the Arctic Thighs took over. If you tried *reading* them files instead of looking for big red clues, you'd figure out Klugman's got something on the side and his wife suspects. Why would she be calling him every hour except to check up on him? Who hired us, him or his insurance company?"

"The insurance company. But—"

"There you go. His new squeeze has got expensive tastes, or else he's busy salting a secret bank account before Mrs. Klugman serves him on an infidelity rap and freezes his assets. That takes dough, so he boosts his own merchandise and sells it down the road, then pockets the insurance payoff. What you got to do is tail him, take pictures. Dollars to dogshit something soft and pink with a high voice comes out of the soup, and it won't be Pee-Wee Herman."

"You mean, er—"

"The old Beautyrest Bolero, the snooper's best friend. Only you better develop them yourself or have a custom place do it, because Fotomat won't. Show 'em to Klugman. He'll confess to the San Francisco earthquake to keep them out of his wife's hands."

"Mrs. Lovechild says—"

"Whose name goes on the report, yours or hers?"

"Mine, but—"

Ralph put a hand on Chuck's shoulder. "Two rules to live by, kid: clients pay for results, and there's always a broad in it somewhere. Find her, get the goods, get paid. Client's happy,

Goosey Lucy's happy, you're happy. Integrity just makes everybody sore."

"I guess it can't hurt to keep an eye on Klugman for a day or so."

"That'll be enough, believe me. If this guy could keep it in his pants that long he wouldn't be in the fix he's in."

"I hope you're right."

"Instincts. They're what put me where I am."

"In the file room?"

"In the numero-uno spot, best private star in town. Well, except for this one-man show over on West Grand River, but he's a Boy Scout."

"Gee, thanks, Mr. Poteet. I don't know why Mrs. Lovechild says you're a pain in the ass."

"She kids a lot. You got change for a twenty?"

Chuck took out his wallet. "All I got's a ten and a five."

"That's okay, you can owe me." Ralph took the bills.

"Where's the twenty?"

"I left my wallet home. Hell, I guess that makes us even."

Ralph continued down the corridor to the file room, mildly ashamed of himself. It was like hunting in the Detroit Zoo.

The room was lead-lined and had no windows. One wall was taken up by built-in file drawers, a third of them empty now that Lucille had hired a crew to transfer everything to computer disks. His desk was a cracked-oak veteran of Eagle Eye, with a matching chair that wailed in mortal agony whenever he turned it and the only black rotary-dial telephone left in southeastern Michigan. First thing, he looked inside the wastebasket and was not surprised to find that his fifth of Four Roses had been confiscated. Shaking his head, he unscrewed his pocket flask and swigged Smirnoff's. Only a wimp was afraid to mix his drinks.

Ralph was the second child of an Ohio Baptist minister and a church secretary, who had picked up and left when Ralph was ten, taking with her the collection for a new church roof and an organist named Donald. Ralph's father never believed Ralph was his son after that and took to beating him with the family Bible (which Ralph always said beat no book-learning at all), once fetching him a blow that detached the retina of his right eye, leaving it sightless and causing it to resemble a sourball that had been sucked and then spat out. When Ralph's sister Ethel was sixteen she had driven across the county line with an assistant supermarket manager named Zwingler and gotten married, but Ralph's father had gone after them with a .410 shotgun and had the marriage annulled. Ralph was fifteen the Thanksgiving Day his father and Ethel got into a serious altercation about the proper way to carve a turkey and she started carving the old man instead, killing him and totally ruining a Black & Decker Floating Wonder cordless electric knife. A court-appointed psychiatrist had pronounced her mentally unfit to stand trial, after which she was committed to the state hospital for the criminally insane. Ralph never visited her, but received a Christmas card from her every August.

His father having had no other relatives, and his mother having last been heard from in 1957 singing in a roadhouse outside Wichita to the intimate accompaniment of Donald's organ, Ralph had been placed in a group home. Two days before his eighteenth birthday, when he would have been given the choice of staying or leaving, he had flushed his group father's teeth down the toilet in the upstairs bathroom and walked out. He had been on his own ever since, not counting a total of three weeks served in jail for failure to register for the draft and obstruction of justice reduced from assaulting an officer after he had sat on one of the policemen summoned to investigate a domestic disturbance between Ralph and his wife.

The judge had released him from custody on the latter complaint in return for Ralph's promise to seek psychiatric counseling. The counselor, a tan and sandy psychiatrist in his thirties with leather patches on his elbows and a Harvard rowing trophy in a glass case in his office, had listened to Ralph's account of his early life and declared that Ralph was the way he was because the Bible beatings had caused him to give up on trying to please his father sooner than most. Flushing his group father's teeth down the toilet was a symbolic castration of his male parent, with a subconscious wish to prevent his own birth. His refusal to register for the draft represented rebellion against authority, born of his inability to defend himself against child abuse, and sitting on the police officer indicated a severe anal fixation; he postulated that Ralph had been constipated for a long time as a result of his father's grisly death at a family dinner. Ralph stole the electric typewriter from the psychiatrist's reception room on his way out and didn't go back for a second session.

At that point, Ralph might have chosen crime as his vocation had he not acquired a violent distaste for jail. He had thought his intimate knowledge of the workings of the dishonest mind ideal for detective work, but knew that his record would not allow him into the police training program in Detroit, where he went to change his luck without stopping off at home to pack or say goodbye to his wife. Insurance work looked close and easy, so he used his new typewriter to draft letters of reference and forged the signatures of Red Adair, Greta Garbo, and George Plimpton, on the theory that these three would be impossible to reach for confirmation, and sent copies along with a wonderfully creative résumé to the three largest insurance companies in Michigan. All three rejected him, so he submitted the material to Great Lakes Universal Life, Casualty, Auto, and Paternity, headquartered above Arnie's Little Touch of Albania Chop House on Livernois in Detroit. There he was interviewed by Arnie himself, smelling of Brut and fried onions, who clamped a greasy hand around his and welcomed him to the firm as a claims adjuster. He worked in that capacity for three years until a series of unfortunate incidents forced his dismissal. If not for Gus Lovechild, who took him on at Eagle Eye as an employee and finally as an uncredited partner,

Ralph would likely be busing tables at the Soup Kitchen or building roads with a work gang in Marquette. He wasn't so sure that both alternatives weren't preferable to juggling files for Lucille. Damn Gus for dying anyway.

When the flask was empty, he stopped reminiscing, took his feet off the desk, and did some filing. The stack of folders atop the desk was not very high and contained nothing in the way of what he considered useful information. He suspected Lucille of culling the choicer bits and locking them in her office so he couldn't get at them. He stuck the folders in their proper drawers, more or less, and sat until noon, idly blacking out teeth in the photograph of Lucille on the desktop advertising calendar she gave to satisfied clients. Then he went to lunch.

His favorite bar was the Vinegaroon on Cass, but that was too far to walk in the drizzling rain that had just started, and anyway the place hadn't been the same since the owner defaulted on a loan payment and wound up hanging by his beer pulls. Florentino's was closest, but Ralph owed Tino money, and lately there had been too many potted ferns and well-dressed men hanging around the Macedonian Room to suit him. He stood deliberating in the rain for a moment with his Tyrolean tugged down, then said to hell with it and trotted across two streets and around a corner to Richard's, wedged between a Cambodian restaurant and an auto parts store that gave discounts to customers with spiked gloves. The furnace worked.

"Hey, Ralph. Same as always?" As usual Richard, the one-armed black bartender who pretended to own the place for a Sicilian named Sal the Hippo, shared the establishment with the Doberman and the guy in the back booth who never ordered anything but Pepto-Bismol and sat making marks in a twelve-year-old *TV Guide* from morning until closing.

"Double it." Ralph climbed onto one of the cleaner stools. The Doberman, whose name was Coleman, raised its chin from its paws on a filthy rug behind the bar, studied Ralph, farted, and went back to sleep.

Ralph fanned away the stink as Richard set a shot of Four Roses and a glass of Budweiser in front of him. "That as dangerous as that mutt gets?"

"I got to stop feeding him cabbage."

Ralph downed the shot and chased it with a slug of beer. "Hit me again."

"I'm surprised you come down from last night. You really tied one on." He refilled the shot glass.

"I was in here?"

"Don't you remember? You bought a Pepto-Bismol for Andy there."

Ralph looked over his shoulder at the guy in the back booth, who was talking to himself now. "He the one I made the bet with?"

"What bet?"

He turned back. "Did I make a call from here?"

"I don't know how you could. Ma Bell took out the phone two years ago. Nobody ever used it."

"I go out around midnight?"

"Man, it was past midnight when you come in."

"Did I say where I was before?"

Richard shook his head.

"Shit."

"Jesus, that must be scary. Losing a whole night."

"Naw. I lost all of 1976." He knocked back the drink and chased it. "Hit me."

"You missed the Bicentennial?"

Ralph watched him pour. "How'd you lose the arm, anyway?"

"Streetcar. How'd you lose the eye?"

"I got a hard-on and looked down too quick."

The telephone behind the bar rang. Ralph said, "I thought you said they took it out."

"This one's mine." Richard answered it. Putting a hand over the mouthpiece: "You here for a guy named O'Leary?"

Ralph took the receiver. "How'd you find me?"

"Your boss gave me a list." The connection seemed to smell of smoke. "Can you swing by police headquarters? I got some more questions."

"Like what?"

"Like who was sore enough at Lyla Dane to try to fry her. It's arson now. But you better come quick, or you could be talking to somebody else."

"How come?"

"If she dies it's homicide. That's how come."

Ralph said he'd be there and gave the receiver back to the bartender. "Shit."

"Bad news?"

"I just remembered why I don't like coming here. Something bad always happens."

Coleman the Doberman farted.

Richard waved at the fumes with the bar rag. "Tomorrow he goes on wintergreen."

Chapter 6

"*W*ho're you now, Boris Karloff?"

O'Leary grunted and waved Ralph into a chair. The arson investigator's desk, all four edges of which were scalloped with burn marks, supported a pair of fat dry-cell batteries the size of Thermos jugs, wired to what appeared to be an ordinary wall switch without a strike plate. The switch was screwed to two wooden uprights nailed to the pine board upon which the dry cells stood. It looked like a high school science project.

"I had the lab fix this up," O'Leary said. "Saves a lot of explaining. This thing here is an arc switch. Know what that is?"

"Golly, gee, no, Mr. Wizard. What is it?"

"You're a card, Poteet. You don't see these much anymore. They've been replaced by more expensive units with less conductible materials for reasons of safety. This one's a duplicate of the one we found installed next to the door of Lyla Dane's apartment. The original burned, of course. But not enough to disguise what it is."

"I'm starting to get it," Ralph said, interested now.

"Really? You're smarter than you—well, than I thought. Anyway, we asked the landlord about it. He said the switches are identical throughout the building. We checked out the one in that empty apartment you and I were in this morning. It's a conventional safety switch, not an arc. He swears the last switch he replaced was in the furnace room, and he did *that* more than six months ago. It isn't an arc either. We checked."

"You're saying somebody snuck in and switched switches."

"You put things cute. But yeah. Then, just before our friend left, he or she turned on all the gas burners on the kitchen range and blew out the pilots. The lady's out for the evening, which is what she does to eat. By the time she gets home, the place is full of fumes. She opens the door, turns on the light—" He flipped the switch. A blue spark crackled between the points.

Ralph said, "Kaboom."

"More like *foom*. Only she weighs less than a hundred pounds, so instead of blowing her to smithereens the blast throws her across the hall, which is what saved her life, for the time being. The report from Ann Arbor isn't good. She's in a coma with third-degree burns over forty percent of her body." He lifted a smoldering cigarette butt from a charred groove on the edge of his desk and inhaled.

Ralph sat back quickly. In the smoke he thought he saw Carpenter's emaciated features. *Watch him while I go up and make sure we didn't forget anything.* "So what'd you pull me down here for? I call the electrician when a bulb needs changing."

O'Leary said nothing for a moment. His big scorched-looking face with its squinched nose was as calm as a morgue slab. Finally he wiped his eyes.

"Yeah. I wanted to ask you face to face what kind of guy this landlord is."

"Vinnie's a sleaze."

"You don't like him?"

"I didn't say that. I had anything against sleazes I wouldn't have no friends at all."

"You're friends?"

"I didn't say that either."

O'Leary flipped his butt disgustedly into a plastic wastebasket by the desk. Leaning over, Ralph saw that it was half-filled with water. Somebody had been with him awhile. "Reason I'm asking, I didn't like the way he acted when we asked him if anybody had been in the apartment last night or this morning besides Lyla Dane."

"What'd he say?"

"He said he didn't know, what'd he look like, some kind of weirdo peeping Tom?"

"Did you tell him?"

"He was lying. You get a sense for it in this work. Thing is, is he protecting himself or somebody else?"

"Vinnie wouldn't stick his fat neck out for Mother Teresa. You sweat him?"

"As far as possible without hauling him in. Reason I called you, everybody we talked to said you were living in the building when they moved in. I figured you'd know him better than any of them."

"I pay my rent, he lets me go on living there. That's about it."

"What about the two guys you were with this morning?"

Ralph reached for a Blue Diamond matchstick to cover the fact that he'd jumped. So O'Leary was that kind of cop. "Talk to Mrs. Gelatto, did you?"

"Should we?"

Dammit. He didn't know now if O'Leary had spoken to her or to the cop who had grilled him in Carpenter's car. "I had a little too much to drink last night," he said. "Looks like I took a couple of guys back to my place for a nightcap when the bar closed. I seen them out around four."

"Names?"

He shrugged. "You drink?"

"I've been known."

"Everybody's your friend. You don't waste time with names."

"What bar were you in?"

"Place called Richard's, for a little. I don't know about before and after."

"Sounds like you got a problem."

"I ain't an alcoholic."

"I mean as to being able to account for your movements last night. Nobody knows what time Lyla Dane went out. You could have rigged the switch and the gas before or after going to this Richard's."

"Could of. If I had a reason."

"There are plenty of reasons when a hooker gets hurt. Maybe she was blackmailing you." Ralph laughed. O'Leary looked sheepish. "Yeah, right. But if I were you, I'd find those friends."

"What makes me your yellow dog?"

"For one thing, not telling me about them in the first place. Strangers in the building on the morning a tenant gets blown up are worth mentioning."

"I didn't figure there was a connection. I still don't. What's another?"

"I don't like you."

"I ain't crazy about you neither."

"I can live with it." O'Leary flipped the switch off and on and off again. "For the record, it was Mrs. Gelatto told us about the three of you on the stairs. In between stories about her late husband and the marvelous curative properties of pickles."

"Maybe we should try them. Can I go now?"

"I got a Mass to go to anyway. Let us know if you have any plans to leave town. You know that song."

Ralph stood. "What kind of Mass takes place in the middle of the week?"

"It's a memorial service. The pastor of my wife's church died sometime last night. They found him this morning in his bed in the rectory. You all right?"

Ralph coughed and spat splinters into the wastebasket. "Yeah. That's the second time today I swallowed one of the bastards. What'd you say your pastor's name was?"

"I didn't. But it was Breame, John Breame. He was a monsignor at St. Balthazar. Sure you're okay?"

"I may start smoking again." He went out.

"New rule, Poteet," said Lucille Lovechild. "No more two-and-a-half-hour lunches."

Anita had shunted him straight into the office with one of her Cheshire grins. Ralph said, "I had to see a man about a fire."

"Interesting you should use that word."

"Man?"

"Fire. Get back to work."

He stopped at Anita's desk. She was still reading *Working Woman*.

"Ain't that like a monk with a subscription to *Playboy*?"

"Why not?" she said. "I bet he gets lucky more often than you do."

"Chuck Waverly around?"

"He went out a little while ago with his camera. Lucille gave you hell, huh? Tell me everything." She closed the magazine and cupped her chin in her palm.

"Well, I hope he took the right film. Them forty-watt bulbs they put in motel rooms can barely light themselves." He turned to go.

"Oh, this came for you by messenger." She held up an envelope.

Ralph didn't take it. "Any windows?"

"No windows."

"My wife's handwriting?"

"I wouldn't know it."

"Jake Otero serves papers in a messenger's uniform. Was he a little round guy with a stupid face?"

"You're a little round guy with a stupid face."

He took it. The envelope was heavy white stock, addressed in fine copperplate. " 'Mr. Ralph Poteet,' " he read aloud.

"A stranger, obviously."

He opened it.

Dear Mr. Poteet:

   If it is not inconvenient, your presence in my home this evening at six o'clock could prove to your advantage and mine.

> Cordially,
> Philip Steelcase
> Bishop-in-Ordinary

A card with a Farmington Hills address engraved on it was clipped to the letter, along with a crisp one-hundred-dollar bill.

"IRS, I hope?" Anita inquired.

"Religious mail." He refolded the bill inside the letter and stuck it in a pocket.

She opened her magazine. "They're way too late."

Chapter 7

"Go away."

"That's no way to talk to a partner," Ralph said.

"Ex-partner. You got the boot and I did too. Now I'm giving it to you. Go away."

Neal English was an independent insurance actuary with an office in the City National Bank Building overlooking Cadillac Square. He had a monolithic face, all planes and angles with fierce black eyebrows like Lincoln's, creating an effect he tried to soften with pink shirts and knobby knitted ties. It was just past five o'clock and he was standing behind his desk, scooping papers into a maroon leather attaché case with gold fittings.

"The boot didn't hurt you none," Ralph said.

"Not a bit. It just cost me my wife and my kid and seven years' seniority at Great Lakes. I'd be running the place now."

"Which one, the insurance company or the Albanian restaurant?"

"Go away, Ralph."

"Hell, Neal, it was a sweet setup. Forge the old coot's signature and slip the policy into the files. Who knew the widow would turn yellow and spill the works? You know what an eighteen-year-old broad could do with half of fifty grand?"

"You could have told Arnie I didn't know anything about it. He damn near prosecuted."

"Well, he didn't, so what's the beef?"

"I was out of work for a year. My wife divorced me and took my boy to Hawaii. I haven't seen either of them in eleven years."

Ralph rested a ham on a corner of the desk. "Kids are expensive to raise, then they turn out crummy anyway. Wives too. Why buy a lake when you can dip your line for free?"

When he came to, he was on his back on the carpet. Neal was sitting on the desk corner Ralph had vacated, sucking his knuckles.

"What do you want, Ralph?"

"You been working out." He sat up, tasting blood. "You didn't used to knock me all the way down."

"You weren't so fat and slow then. Don't get up yet; I've got another hand. What do you want?"

"I think somebody's out to kill me."

"Tell whoever it is I said good luck."

"I ain't kidding."

"Me neither."

"You know that hooker got blown up this morning?"

"The gas explosion? I read about it."

"Well, it wasn't no accident."

"You blew up a hooker?"

"Hell no. What do I look like?"

"Right now, a pile of shit on my rug."

"It was in my building. Somebody let himself in, monkeyed with the wall switch so it'd throw a spark, and filled the place with gas on his way out."

"Brainy. What was the hooker into and what was your angle?"

"It's more like who was into the hooker." Ralph told him the rest, beginning with Lyla Dane's call and finishing with the discovery of the arc switch. He left out the part about the photographs.

"This the same Monsignor John Breame the *News* said was found by an altar boy counting angels in his bed at the St. Balthazar rectory this morning?" Neal asked.

"Thanks to me and this bug Carpenter."

"So?"

"The blowup was meant for me, ain't that obvious? Carpenter assumed I'd be going back to that same apartment and rigged it while I was waiting for him down on the street. Only I didn't go there. I went back to my place and went to bed."

"Bishops don't kill people over priests that can't keep their vows in their pants."

Ralph sucked on his split lip. "What world you living in, Neal? Shape the Catholic Church is in, he might do just that to keep it quiet."

"Count yourself lucky, then. Justice passed you by this time. You've screwed more people than any ten hookers."

"Thing is, I got an appointment with the bishop in less than an hour. Could be he wants to finish the job."

"Don't go."

"I got to. Could be I got some business there."

Neal slid off the desk. "Get up, Ralph."

"You told me not to."

"I changed my mind. Get up."

"If I do you'll just knock me down again."

"That's the idea. Scamming the Church, Jesus. What'd you do, take pictures?"

"Just half a roll. They got all the money in the world, why shouldn't I get some of it?"

"Ask the hooker."

"All I want you to do is hold the film for me. It could be what keeps me alive."

"That's not an argument in its favor."

"Come on, Neal. I always said you had a heart as big as your ass."

"I've been working out, remember? They're neither of them as big as they used to be. But I'll hold the film."

Ralph grinned. "Hey, I knew you would."

"Just cut me in for half."

"Half of what?"

"Half of whatever the bishop pays you for the film. If I think you're cheating me I'll drop a dime on you, tell him you squirreled away extra negatives to squeeze him with later."

"He'd have that bastard Carpenter chop me down for spite!"

"Good a reason as any. Half's the price; take it or leave it."

"Come on, Neal. That ain't your style."

"It is today."

"You ain't the only friend I got."

"You don't even have me. If you had anyone else to go to, you wouldn't be here bleeding all over your shirt."

"Half. Don't nobody in this town know any other fractions?" He dug the container out of his pocket and held it up. Neal took it.

"Can I get up now?"

"Sure."

Ralph got up. Neal hit him with his other fist. Ralph fell back against a wall, knocking loose a framed bar graph depicting the probable life spans of men and women based on environment, ratio of height to weight, and number of vices. Ralph stood at the low end. He put a hand to his nose and looked at the blood. "What the hell was *that* for?"

"Old times' sake. When you going to check in?"

He found his handkerchief and dabbed at his nose. "Around eight. I'll call from my place. They got the fire out before it reached my floor."

"That was lucky. Gin flames are the hardest to put out."

Ralph left, tipping his head back with the handkerchief wadded under his nostrils. He drove across town with one hand on the wheel and the other at his nose. His lip had begun to swell.

Outside the city limits, his route took him around and between steep hills with houses set into them like precious stones on green felt. The rain had let up and the sun had come out, making the smooth lawns sparkle. Bishop Steelcase's street was a winding cul-de-sac lined with ranch houses, colonials, and large rambling English Tudors, at the end of which stood a big house built of gray stone with a slate roof and coach lamps flanking the front door. Blood-red firebushes grew to the sills of the ground-floor windows.

His nose had stopped bleeding. Waiting for someone to answer the bell, he scrubbed the last traces from his nostrils and folded the handkerchief into a pocket.

"Poteet."

Standing in the open doorway, Carpenter looked even more like a martyr than he had that morning in Lyla Dane's apartment. He had on the same black coat buttoned to the neck and the light behind him haloed his stubbled head.

Ralph shrank back. "I didn't think you'd be here."

"His Excellency is expecting you."

"People know where I am."

"I'm glad for you." He stepped aside.

Ralph entered a foyer hung with medieval tapestries and followed Carpenter down a hallway paneled in worm-eaten oak that looked as old as the Crusades. At the end Carpenter knocked on a cherrywood door. A voice invited them inside.

The bishop was a tall old man, nearly as thin as Carpenter, with white hair brushed back in creamy waves and a face dark as hickory and falling away to the white shackle of his clerical collar. He rose from behind a mahogany desk, wearing a black cassock that swept to the floor and made him look like something not bound to the earth. The room was large and square and smelled of pipe tobacco and leather from the books on the built-in shelves. A large crucifix carved from a single block of wood hung on the wall behind the desk. Carpenter entered behind Ralph and closed the door.

"Thank you for coming, Mr. Poteet," said the bishop. "Please sit down."

"Thank Ben Franklin." But he settled into a deep leather chair that gripped his buttocks like a big hand in a soft glove. He kept his hat on.

"Have you been in an accident?"

"Just my face."

The bishop lowered himself into the big swivel chair behind the desk, his back as straight as the crucifix.

"I'm grateful for this opportunity to thank you in person for your discretion this morning," he said. "The Church has few enough friends this season. Are you by any chance Catholic?"

"Nope. Too much kneeling."

The bishop nodded as if in agreement. "I'm very disappointed with Monsignor Breame. I'd hoped he would assume my post at the head of the diocese."

"I guess he thought he found a better place to put his post."

"Yes. Well, now I must begin the process all over again."

"You bucking for cardinal?"

He smiled. "I suppose you've shown yourself worthy of some confidence. As a matter of fact, His Holiness did say something about the red hat in my presence during his visit here last month. Of course, it's far from official."

"I bet you got your plane ticket and everything."

"Don't interrupt His Excellency."

"It's all right, Carpenter. If I weren't patient I'd hardly be a candidate."

Ralph said, "Your right bower cashing in his chips in some hooker's bed wouldn't sit so good with Rome, I bet. I guess that's why you tried to croak me."

"What do you mean?"

"Carpy there didn't do his homework. Thought I was Lyla's pimp or something instead of her neighbor and that I shared her apartment. Which he rigged to blow up in my face, only it blew up in hers instead."

"What is he talking about?"

"There was a fire after I left," Carpenter said. "The woman was hurt. I heard it on the news."

"Do you know anything about it?"

"Oh, Christ," Ralph said. "Excuse my French."

"The building is a firetrap, Your Excellency. Anything could have started it."

"Cops found the arc switch." Ralph crossed his legs, drawing a farting noise out of the leather. "I took pictures. They're with a friend. You know how that goes."

"Extortion, Mr. Poteet?"

"Let's just call it blackmail. I ain't dressed good enough for extortion."

One corner of the desk supported a silver tray containing two long-stemmed glasses and a cut-crystal decanter half-filled with ruby liquid. The bishop removed the stopper and filled both glasses.

"This is a good port. I confess that the austere life allows me two mild vices. The other is tobacco."

"What are we celebrating?" Ralph didn't touch either glass.

"Your new appointment as chief of diocesan security. The position pays well and the hours are regular."

Ralph had a sudden urge to rub his hands together. He resisted it. "Who do I answer to, Carpenter?"

"Carpenter works for me. The security chief works without supervision. You would have a separate office in the St. Balthazar rectory."

"In return for which I come down with amnesia?"

"And entrust all related material to me, naturally." The bishop sipped from his glass.

Ralph lifted his then. "What's to stop me from becoming Shake 'n' Bake like Lyla?"

"Neither Carpenter nor I had anything to do with that. You have a very dark view of religion."

"Must be all them pictures I seen of eyes getting put out and Protestants burning at the stake." He gulped off half his wine. It tasted bitter.

"Do you know Bibles, Mr. Poteet?"

"I knew my old man's pretty good."

The bishop laid a bony hand atop an ancient ornate Bible on the desk. Ralph thought he was about to swear his innocence. "This one belonged to St. Thomas. More, not Aquinas. I have a weakness for religious antiquities."

"Thought you only had two vices." Ralph's fat lip was getting in the way of his speech.

"I would call it more of an obsession. My colleagues think my ambition is motivated by power, or piety, if they are charitable. Neither assumption is correct. When I think of the Vatican, its glorious age and awesome history, of enjoying access daily to Constantinople's manuscripts, the pallet where Hadrian the First laid his head, the Sistine ceiling—"

"Careful there, Reverend. You're getting drool on the Gideon."

Bishop Steelcase lifted his hand in a gesture almost of benediction. "Do you accept the position?"

"Trouble with church offices is they all smell like galoshes. Tell you what: you put me on retainer, say a couple of thousand a month, and I keep the pictures."

"That won't do. They must be part of the package."

"Well, you're shit out of luck. 'Scuse my Flen—French." The air in the room was thickening. He could scarcely breathe through his sore nose.

"Your Excellency?"

"Not yet, Carpenter."

Ralph's grin seemed to spill all over his face. He dumped the rest of his wine into it. "Don't feel too bad, Parson. You ain't the first Holy Joe somebody's had over the altar." His vision was blurring. He was beginning to think there was something to that business about not mixing the grape with the grain.

"The crucifix on that wall is said to have hung in Charlemagne's palace at Constantinople," the bishop was saying. "In any case, the experts I had examine it agree that it dates back at least as far as the tenth century. Are you all right, Mr. Poteet? I fear my collection is putting you to sleep."

Ralph could no longer see the crucifix. Both the bishop and Carpenter were shimmering shadows. He leaned forward to return his glass to the tray and kept going, to the floor.

He thought, shit, I bet this means no job neither.

Chapter 8

*H*e awoke feeling pretty much the way he did most mornings, with his head throbbing and a tongue the size of a ham. His eyes were painted shut.

When he got them open, he thought he'd lost the sight in his good eye. Then, as the pupil let in light from a corner streetlamp, he saw the dashboard in front of him and realized that night had fallen and he was sitting on the passenger's side of the red Riviera. Then he felt a tug and a chill and looked down to see that his pants were down around his ankles. Something in three sweaters and a man's felt hat was on the floor trying to work them off over his shoes.

"Hey."

The brim of the hat came up. Under it was a face fashioned from dirty clay, vaguely female, with large nostrils, eyes shot pink, and six amber teeth in a black hole of mouth. Gray hair straggled down on either side. Ralph smelled half-digested gin.

"I figured you was dead," said the creature.

"Well, I ain't."

"You sure? I seen dead cats get up and walk away 'cause nobody told them."

"Not between bottles you didn't. You want to let go of my pants?"

"You don't need pants if you're dead."

"Old lady, you don't neither."

She sat back on her heels. "Well, why'd you park here if you ain't dead? This ain't no place to be alive in."

"What place is it?"

"Mount Elliott Cemetery."

"Jesus. You sure it ain't Farmington Hills?"

She cackled. It sounded like someone pulling nails. "Well, now, I guess it might be at that. And this here's beef Wellington for supper." She pulled a dead rat out of a sweater pocket and dangled it by its tail.

"You going to *eat* that?" He shrank from it.

"I'll let you have a bite if you'll give me them pants."

He bent down to pull them up. Blackness overtook him and he grabbed the dash to keep from rapping his head against it. The glove compartment popped open. The old woman lunged for the flat pint bottle that came sliding out, but he caught it first. He unscrewed the cap and took a long pull. As the heat climbed his belly, he thought about Neal English expecting his call at eight o'clock and peered at his wrist in the moonlight. It was bare.

"Gimme my watch."

"Ain't got no watch." The old woman's face became a caricature of craft.

He held out the bottle. When she grasped at it, he hung on. She shrugged, mounted an excavation inside her clothes, and came up with Ralph's Timex.

"Takes a licking and keeps on ticking. Only it don't keep time for shit." She held it against her breasts.

Ralph proffered the bottle again. "One swallow."

She gave him the watch then and took the bottle in both hands. He held on while she tilted it. The bourbon spilled over her chin and down inside her sweaters. He wrenched it free, started to lift it again to his lips, looked at the neck, and gave it to her. In seconds she and the bottle were gone out the open door on the driver's side.

He put on the watch and turned its face into the light. It read 8:37. "Shit." He pulled up his pants carefully, noticing as he did so that two of the pockets were turned out, slid over behind the wheel, and slammed the door. The key was in the ignition. He started the motor and turned on the lights. In front of him a large headstone sprang into view reading FUCHT. He swung the car out into Mt. Elliott Street. It was one of Detroit's worst blocks, home to street gangs, crack peddlers, and prostitutes, a far cry from Bishop Steelcase's study. Even Carpenter must have stepped lively after driving Ralph all that way.

Ralph's thoughts were still fuzzy. Whatever the bishop had slipped him, it must have been in the hollow stem of his glass before it was filled, because Ralph had been watching him too closely during the pouring and had waited until the bishop drank from his own glass before committing himself. He didn't know what they had thought to accomplish by drugging him, but he wished he knew what the stuff was called, because it had restored his memory. He now knew every place he'd been the night before. As it turned out, he'd had a great time.

He drove several blocks before he found a telephone that looked safe, inside the entrance of a drugstore that was offering a ten percent rebate on condoms and pantyhose. He parked the Riviera where he could keep an eye on it and called Neal's office. When there was no answer he got his home number from Information.

"Hello?"

"Neal, this is Ralph."

"Go away."

"Quit kidding around. You didn't send that stuff to the cops yet, did you?"

"What stuff?"

"The film, for chrissake!"

"Oh, that. No, I still got it."

"Jesus, that's a relief. How come?"

"How come what?"

"If you didn't hear from me by eight you were supposed to send the film to the cops. What stopped you?"

"You didn't say that."

"I didn't figure I had to. That's the whole reason I had you hold it, in case someone wanted to croak me."

"You don't sound croaked."

"That ain't the point! What's the good of having somebody hold the evidence if he don't do like he's supposed to?"

"You get the money?"

"I got doped."

"The bishop slipped you a mickey?"

"There I was, guzzling wine and talking about Charlemagne, and the next thing I know a bag lady's taking off my pants in the cemetery."

"Just like in the public-service announcements."

"Listen, if you don't hear from me in twenty-four hours, stick that film in an envelope and send it to a guy named O'Leary at police headquarters. He's with Arson."

"When do I get my cut?"

"Neal, if it comes to you sending O'Leary that film, I'll be too dead to give it to you."

"Hell, I can't lose." The line clicked and buzzed.

Ralph hung up, turned to leave, then remembered Vinnie. The landlord had given him until that night to decide whether to cut him in on his action, then he was going to the cops. Ralph dialed the adult bookstore, then Vinnie's apartment. He let both phones ring eighteen times before giving up.

Vinnie never left the building and rarely ventured above the ground floor. Where could he be?

"The cophouse." Ralph hurried out of the drugstore and spun the Riviera's wheels.

Vinnie didn't own a car—had never learned to drive, in fact, and was too cheap to ride in taxis. Buses didn't run at night. If he was on his way to Detroit Police Headquarters on Beaubien, Ralph would see him on the street. He took that route to his building.

None of the pedestrians he spotted on the way had Vinnie's bald head or cartoony walk. Ralph thought he saw him once, but it turned out to be an inflatable doll someone had leaned against a pile of garbage bags on John R. The streets were full of bums with bladder-control problems—Christmas was too far away for them to be called "the homeless"—and youths looking for telephone booths to vandalize. The bad element stayed indoors during brisk weather.

The bookstore was dark, with the Closed sign in the window over Harry Reems's crotch. Ralph pulled into the space where Carpenter's station wagon had been early that morning and bounded into the foyer next door. The security buzzer hadn't worked since Nixon.

The door to Vinnie's apartment was locked. Ralph knocked, waited, then slipped the lock with the celluloid window from his wallet that displayed a picture of Tom Wopat. The layout consisted of a bedroom, bathroom, and living room with kitchenette—sparsely furnished, almost antiseptically clean, and containing nothing that couldn't appear in a Disney film. At work in the bookstore, Vinnie read Fu Manchu novels and played one-handed pinochle. The smart money in the building said he had never had his cork popped, nor wanted to. Vinnie's wife was in California six months out of the year, making 16-mm films for the Battlefield Production Company and posing for those ballpoint pens that presented lessons in the female anatomy when turned upside down. Ralph could only guess at their relations when they shared the place.

No Vinnie.

Ralph drank a bottle of Bartles & Jaymes wine cooler he found in the refrigerator, helped himself to a cut-crystal salt shaker Vinnie would never miss, and sat down to think. The residue of the bishop's wine made his thoughts come slowly and in ragged order, like a line of cars crossing a stop street. It wasn't like Vinnie to go to the cops without hearing from Ralph first. It wasn't like Vinnie to go to the cops, period; especially when there was money to be made by not going. Not doing something and getting paid for it was Landlords' Heaven.

Wondering if he might be in Lyla Dane's apartment figuring how to jack up the damages for the insurance company, Ralph mined himself out of the horsehair sofa, locked up (the building was full of thieves), and climbed the stairs to the third floor. The hallway smelled of smoke and firemen's rubber boots.

No Vinnie there either. The door to the apartment, what was left of it, was closed, with a yellow seal taped across it reading POLICE CRIME SCENE—KEEP OUT.

Ralph went down to his floor. There was a chance Vinnie was waiting for him in his apartment. He wouldn't even really need his passkey, thanks to Tyrell the fireman and his little chop for whores.

Ralph's first thought when he opened the shattered door was that he hadn't noticed how messy his housekeeping had gotten lately. Then he saw the stuffing from the slashed sofa cushions among the broken, torn, and overturned bric-a-brac, and he mulled that over for a drug-induced minute. Very slowly he remembered finding his pockets turned out in Mt. Elliott Cemetery, and the way the disarranged contents of his glove compartment had spat out the pint of bourbon when the lid popped open. The bag lady wouldn't have done all that without taking the bottle and his wallet.

oooooo

Carpenter would have.

He knew then why he'd been drugged.

At that moment, a lucid Ralph would have started running and not stopped this side of Eight Mile Road. For all Carpenter's resemblance to a Christian from the catacombs, he would not be likely to forgive being interrupted before finishing the job Vinnie had started. A befogged Ralph looked around for a weapon. He hadn't seen his revolver since August, when it came back from the gunsmith's shop with new grips after that time he'd caught it on an escalator railing at the Northland Hudson's and almost shot off his right ham. He pulled the loose leg off the capsized coffee table, fisting it like a club, and charged into the bedroom. Inside the door he tripped, clawed for balance, and knocked himself cold with the makeshift bludgeon.

When he came around moments later, he was staring up at the burning bulb of one of the lamps he had adjusted to illuminate Monsignor Breame during the photo session that morning. It appeared to be glaring back with a cyclopean intensity, and for a moment (it must have been the company he was keeping) he thought that he had come to Judgment. He put a hand down to push himself into a sitting position, stuck it with the nail from the coffee table leg, sucked at the stigmata, and looked at Vinnie. Vinnie was what had tripped him.

The landlord was sprawled on his back on the floor in a cartoon attitude, arms and legs splayed and his sweatshirt ridden up to expose his round hairless belly. His round eyes were wide open, his mouth a perfect O with his tongue sticking out of it, his naked scalp throwing off light from the lamp. A green polyester tie with orange planets on it was knotted around his neck, the knot sunk deep in fat. It was Ralph's lucky tie.

Chapter 9

" '*E*vening, Mrs. Gelatto," Ralph said.

The old woman in the babushka and black leather jacket paused on her way downstairs, fished her glasses out of her purse, and peered through them at Ralph. "Oh, it's you. Who's that with you?"

"Just a friend." He leaned harder into Vinnie's sagging frame to keep it from sliding into a heap on the landing.

"Mr. Capablanca, ain't it?" she said. "You was supposed to come up and fix my faucet a week ago. Don't you stick your tongue out at me, young man."

After removing the strangling necktie with difficulty, Ralph had tried pushing Vinnie's swollen tongue back inside his mouth, but it kept popping out. Ralph said, "He's just got a little stomach flu. I'm taking him out for air."

"Pickles is the thing for that. They absorb all the poisons. Mr. Gelatto—"

"Smelled like Vlasic. You told me, Mrs. Gelatto. Ain't you on your way to work?"

"I know that. I was scrubbing floors when you was crawling on them."

"No argument. Good night, Mrs. Gelatto."

"Terrible thing, what happened to that woman on my floor."

"Sure was. Terrible thing." His shoulder was going to sleep.

"Mr. Gelatto wouldn't have gas in the house. He had plenty in bed, though. It was all them pickles. Hee-hee."

"Ha-ha. Well, good night."

"Get your friend home okay this morning?"

"Yeah. He needed rest, was all. He's resting now."

"Mr. Capablanca don't look no better than he did. You boys got to stop living so high."

"I expect Vinnie will. Good night, Mrs. Gelatto."

"Don't forget that faucet."

"I'll remind him."

She toddled past them and down. Ralph waited until he heard the street door slam, then pulled Vinnie's arm back across his shoulders and descended the stairs a step at a time; his feet first, then Vinnie's. The landlord was a lot lighter than Monsignor Breame, but with the monsignor Ralph had had Carpenter's help. Also, the earlier hour made for more haste if he was to avoid being seen by any more tenants. Mrs. Gelatto didn't count. Ralph had considered waiting past midnight, but he knew the limits of his nerve, and they didn't include a long vigil in his own apartment with a man who had been murdered with Ralph's own necktie. Fortunately, he hadn't as many flights to negotiate this trip. One or two more corpses and he'd have the routine down cold.

He reached the foyer without further incident and parked Vinnie on the bottom step while he used the window from his wallet to slip the lock on Vinnie's door once again. Inside, he dumped the landlord on the living room floor, arranged his arms and legs in roughly the same position he'd found them in, and went through the apartment carefully smearing everything he'd touched on his last visit. Items wiped clean of prints attracted almost as much cop suspicion as a decent print. Reluctantly he took the crystal salt shaker out of his pocket, rubbed it between his palms, and returned it to its place on the table in the dining nook. Someone knocked on the door.

"Mr. Capablanca? Vinnie Capablanca?"

Ralph froze. The voice belonged to O'Leary, the arson investigator.

"Is anybody home?" He knocked again.

Ralph stood over the splayed body, not breathing, as the doorknob began to turn. He couldn't remember if he'd locked the door behind him.

The knob stopped turning. Someone rattled it. After that there was a long silence, during which Ralph wanted a drink. He became nostalgic for the farting dog at Richard's. He was afraid even to shift his weight because of the squeaky floorboards. It would be just like a sneaky cop to slip the lock.

Finally he heard footsteps withdrawing. The staircase creaked as someone climbed it.

Ralph waited another minute, then crept forward and put his good eye to the peephole in the door. The foyer was deserted. Quickly he opened the door and stepped out. O'Leary started back downstairs.

Coughing loudly to cover the noise, Ralph slammed the door. Without pausing he hammered on it. "C'mon, Vinnie, I locked myself out! Vinnie?"

"Nobody's home. I was just there."

Ralph jumped convincingly and turned toward O'Leary. A seam tore; he'd caught one flap of his suitcoat between the door and the frame. He leaned against the door. "I didn't know you was there. I left my key in the apartment."

"You won't need it. I just came from there. One of our boys did a good job on your door." The arson investigator paused on the stairs with his hands in his pockets. The cigarette in his mouth was leaking ash onto his sportcoat, which already had a hole burned in one lapel. "I wanted to ask your landlord what time Miss Dane usually came home. Maybe you can tell me."

Ralph tugged at his coat. It wouldn't budge. "Oh, different times; you know."

"I don't know. That's why I asked."

"Well, you don't set your watch by no whores. Unless you're in bed with them, ha."

"See, that's the problem. If nobody could predict when she'd be out or how long, how'd the torch know when to go in and rig the switch?"

"Yeah. Boy, that's a toughie." With his hidden hand he tried opening the door a crack. It had locked when he slammed it.

"Can we go up to your apartment? I'd like to ask you some more questions."

"Could we make it later? I got a date."

"I thought you were just coming in."

"I was. Standing here waiting for Vinnie I remembered I'm late."

"Another blackout?"

"Nope. Just running behind."

"You been in a fight?"

Ralph touched his fat lip. His nose had stopped bleeding, but he had a knot on his forehead from the coffee table leg. "I took a brodie down the fucking stairs."

"You just got here, you said."

"Not these stairs. Another stairs."

"You ought to leave yourself alone. You find out yet who those friends were this morning?"

"Working on it." Ralph crossed his ankles.

"Hope you come up with something. Listen, I won't keep you."

"I guess I can wait a minute for Vinnie. I'll need that key later and he might be asleep. I guess they need you back at headquarters."

"News to me." The column of ash on O'Leary's cigarette grew long and plopped to his coat. He didn't brush it off. "She might make it, they're saying now."

"Who?"

"Lyla Dane. Doctors say she's holding her own and if that keeps up her chances get better by the minute. Coming out of the coma is something else again."

"That's great. Her maybe making it, I mean."

"Yeah. Listen, I took a look through that hole in your door."

Oh, shit. "Yeah?"

"What made the mess, the explosion or the firemen?"

"Neither. I ain't had much time to tidy up lately."

"You ought to see my rec room. Good name for it." O'Leary came down the rest of the way and grasped the front-door handle. "Hey, what about your tie?"

"Tie?"

"You know, that thing that goes around your neck."

"Neck?"

"I mean, I know times have changed for the kids, but guys like you and me need all the help we can get on dates. They like it when you dress up, no matter what they say."

"Oh." Ralph felt the blood coming back into his face. "This ain't that kind of date."

"Suit yourself." O'Leary snapped away his burning butt. "Let me know when your memory kicks in. You're still on the list."

When he had left, Ralph used the celluloid window again, freed his coat, and mopped his sweat off the doorknob with his handkerchief.

Back in his apartment he drained the last two drops from the gin bottle he'd awakened with that morning—it was the only thing still where he'd left it—and went into the bathroom to splash water on his face. Someone, either Vinnie or his killer, had pulled the broken corner out of the back of the medicine cabinet and failed to replace it.

Two scenarios. Either Vinnie had discovered Carpenter tossing the place and gotten himself throttled for it, or it had happened the other way around when Carpenter came to search for the film and found Vinnie already engaged in the same task. It didn't much matter to Vinnie which way it went. Ralph would miss him. Mrs. Capablanca and Ralph didn't get along, and if Lucille Lovechild was any indication of how widows carried on their late husbands' works, it looked like he'd be changing his address soon. At least he'd get to keep his camera.

If it still worked. Someone had pried open the back, found it innocent of film, and thrown it on the bedroom floor. All Ralph could determine from pressing the button was that the shutter still stuck. He put it in the closet—stripped, like the rest of the room.

Finding the telephone took some doing. The nightstand he kept it on had been dumped over along with his old bureau and his mattress and bedding, and he had to start at the wall and trace the cord to where the instrument lay buried under a pile of underwear, Archie comic books, and two pillows whose slips needed changing. It was squawking, a healthy sign. He worked the plunger and called Neal English at his home.

"Go away, Ralph."

"Neal, I hope you got that film stashed in a safe place."

"You got my cut yet?"

"Not yet, for chrissake. I'm just checking on my insurance. Things are getting heavy."

"That's just your fat butt."

"C'mon, Neal!"

"Don't get your balls in an uproar. I put it in my box at the bank."

"Hey, thanks, buddy."

"I'm not your buddy, asshole. I can't bleed you if I don't take care of the goods." He hung up.

Ralph was feeling better. There would be hell to pay when Vinnie turned up dead, but landlords were nobody's favorite people anyway, and smut peddlers even less so. The list of suspects ranged from a little old lady who couldn't get her faucet fixed to the Pope. Which, come to think of it, wasn't so far off the mark. Mrs. Gelatto had seen Ralph on the stairs with the body, but blind-as-a-bat eyewitnesses were hard to credit. All he had to do was keep his mouth shut. As for Carpenter, now that he knew Ralph didn't carry the film with him or have it hidden in his apartment, Ralph was a lot more dangerous to him dead than alive.

Even so, Ralph spent half an hour looking through the debris for his revolver. It was a piece of junk, an off-brand Italian piece rebored to American .38 caliber that he'd bought for forty dollars from a pawnbroker on Gratiot when he was still working for Great Lakes Universal Life, Casualty, Auto, and Paternity; but with his door in splinters he'd have felt safer with it inside his reach. He couldn't find it, however.

Realizing suddenly that he hadn't had a nibble of anything all day that couldn't be poured into a glass, he scouted out the refrigerator. He came up with a slice of headcheese that had begun to turn blue around the edges and a quart of milk that didn't smell too suspicious. Someone had been in there as well, he was pretty sure; but not looking for food. He stuck the meat between two slices of bread and ate it, washing it down with milk straight from the carton. It had always amazed him how much better barley was than anything else fermented.

He flipped the knob on the TV but got nothing on any channel. Investigating, he discovered that someone had pulled the set away from the wall, unscrewed the back panel, and torn apart the works. After that he went to bed, but before he climbed under the covers he went back into the living room and retrieved the coffee table leg. As a weapon it had proven itself, if only upon him.

○○○○○○

The telephone pulled him out of an erotic dream.

"Whoever you are, you'd better hang up right now, or I'll find out where you live and order a truckload of pigshit and give them your address."

The caller cleared his throat. "Mr. Poteet?"

"Who the hell is this?"

"This is Philip Steelcase."

"Who the hell is Philip Steelcase?"

"Bishop Steelcase, Mr. Poteet. You can't have forgotten."

He sat up, scratched his head, and hung the alarm clock in front of his good eye. "It's almost midnight!" he whined.

"Thank you. I wonder if you could meet me in the St. Balthazar rectory at noon tomorrow."

"And let you slip me another mickey?"

"I regret that very much. If you'll see me, I'll show you just how much."

"What's that supposed to mean?"

"It means you win, Mr. Poteet. I accept your terms. The retainer was two thousand per month, I believe. In any case I should like to discuss the arrangements."

Ralph said he'd be there and fell out of bed, spearing a buttock with the nail attached to the table leg.

Chapter 10

Lucille Lovechild had her glasses off, always a bad sign.
Today she was wearing a steel-gray suit and a navy turtleneck
sweater that made her look like a U-boat commander. She stood
with her fingers spread on her desktop, her usual attitude when
Ralph was in the room.

He said, "Let 'er rip, *Commandante*."

"You are not to talk to any of my operatives."

"I'm one of your operatives."

"You're a file clerk."

"Talk about what?"

"Anything. Politics, religion, the weather, sex, the investigation business, who played Little Luke on *The Real McCoys*."

"Michael Winkleman."

"Who cares? If you see someone in the hall who compli-
ments you on your choice of ties—an unlikely event, granted, but
myopia and electrical blackouts are common hazards—you will
continue past without acknowledgment. I can put it in writing if
you like."

"What's wrong with my tie?" He had put on the lucky one this morning. After having been used as a garrote it was a little wrinkled, but just handling it last night had landed him an endowment of two grand per month—although he was considering asking for more.

She said, "You can wear a boa constrictor around your neck for all I care; in fact, I'd prefer it. I just don't want you associating with any of my people."

"What's this one about?"

"Very early this morning, for the second morning in a row, I was awakened by a telephone call. It was young Chuck Waverly, asking me to come down to the Wayne County Jail and post bail for him. He was under arrest for criminal trespass and assault."

"Who'd he hit?"

"A fist belonging to a guest in room six of the Acre of Ecstasy Motel in East Detroit, repeatedly. The charge of assault in this case refers to invasion of privacy with a camera. It seems that Waverly broke into the room while it was occupied and started taking pictures of the registered guest while *he* was occupying a young woman who gave her name to the police as Tiffany Waterford. It seems you told him to do it."

"If a guy wants to dip his stick, he don't need my advice. If he did, I wouldn't of steered him to a dump like the Acre of Ecstasy. They got that liquid soap there that smells like—"

"I mean Waverly."

"Which one's he, the dumpy guy in back?"

"*You're* the dumpy guy in back. You know very well whom I mean."

"Did he hang on to the camera?"

"What's that got to do with anything?"

"Hell, Lucille—"

"Mrs. Lovechild."

"Hell, Mrs. Lovechild—"

"Don't curse in this office, you son of a bitch."

"Jiminy cricket, Mrs. L., if he got the pictures—"

"Jiminy cricket?"

"If he got the pictures and he hung on to them, you ought to give him a raise. Me, too, for putting him wise. Them shots of Klugman getting his oil changed will clear up that insurance beef like—"

"The pictures he took were of Arthur Hieronymous Blund, midwestern sales representative for the Needleman Farm Implements Corporation of Urbana, Illinois. It was the wrong room. Mr. Blund is threatening to sue."

"Is there a Mrs. Blund?"

"I wouldn't know. I never heard of him until I saw his name on the arrest report."

"If there is, he won't sue. Chances are he won't even if there ain't. He might if the broad's name was anything but Tiffany. Can you picture Judge Wapner hearing that one?"

"I didn't call you in here to collaborate on a what-to-name-the-baby book. From now on Chuck Waverly and everything under this roof with ears to listen to your line of crap are off limits." She sniffed the air. "Have you been drinking?"

"Drinking and stinking." He aimed a matchstick at his mouth and got it on the second try.

"I knew it! You come in here battered up from some barroom brawl, limping—"

"I sat on a nail."

"Take that thing out of your mouth," she said.

"How come?"

"Because I'm going to kiss you, that's how come."

"Jesus, Lucille—I mean, golly gumwart, Mrs. Lovechild, I never figured—" He missed the matchstick and grasped his nose between thumb and forefinger. It wouldn't come loose.

"Never mind. The urge has passed. The reason I wanted to kiss you is you just broke a rule. I gave you till Friday before you broke down on the alcohol thing, but you must think it's my birthday. I've dreamed of saying these words: You're fired."

"I quit."

"No, you're fired."

"Quit."

"Fired."

"I said I quit before you said you're fired."

"You did not. I said you're fired first."

"Yeah, well, you're ugly."

"I beg your pardon?"

"You should. If I had a face like yours I'd shave my ass and walk around on my hands."

She flipped the switch on the intercom. "Anita, call security."

"You want me to tell them to blow the little fucker away?"

"Just call them."

"Soon as she's through Ziebarting her nails," Ralph said. "Anyway, the boys in security already know you're ugly. I bet poor old Gus kicked the bucket before he figured out which end to fuck."

"I'll have your severance check sent to your apartment."

"Keep it."

She blinked. "Keep what?"

"The bucks. The currency. The lucre. The swag. The dough-re-mi. The stuff that dreams are made of."

"Do you mean the money?"

"Sure, I mean the money. Give it to a plastic surgeon. I know one in Ferndale'll cut you a deal on a new honker. He uses those little pieces of Styrofoam that come with Osterizers. Cuts down on the overhead."

"Cancel security." She turned off the intercom in the middle of Anita's disappointed groan. Then she put on her glasses. "When did you start losing interest in cash?"

"When I got a better job. This new one uses my talents."

"Is the circus in town?"

His grin felt lopsided. He was drunker than he'd thought. "You remember the time that truck pulled into your driveway and unloaded forty gross of Popeil potato smashers and six dozen *Slim Whitman Yodels Songs of Faith* albums?"

"It took me a week to get them off my front lawn. How'd *you* know about it?" Realization dawned. "You bastard."

"I thought it was April Fool's Day."

"It was Martin Luther King's birthday. I was seeing an oboist with the Detroit Symphony at the time. He dumped me. It wasn't because of the potato smashers."

"How about the time you stuck your hand into your mailbox and come up with a fistful of live bait?"

"Nothing like that ever happened to me."

"C'mon, it was just last month."

"I don't even *have* a mailbox. I use the post office on the corner."

"Shit. I must of got the address wrong."

"Level with me, Ralph: why did Gus hire you? You're a sleaze and a goof-off and everyone you have any contact with comes to misery. I never met a stick before with *two* shitty ends."

"Gus and me had a lot in common."

"What, two ears and the same shoe size?"

"You wouldn't see it, just being married to him. You never sat in a car with him all night long in front of some blonde's house, drinking coffee out of a Thermos while somebody's husband was inside slam-dunking her between silk sheets. Why'd he pick you, anyway?"

"I showed him which fork to use at a formal dinner party and how to tie a white tie. I took him out of polyester and made a gentleman out of him."

"I got to say he looked damn good laid out in them tweeds."

"He died of trichinosis from the Tuesday special at the House of Pork," she said. "A restaurant you recommended."

"Yeah, I was sorry when they closed the place down. They gave me free meals in the kitchen for sending them business. Not on Tuesdays, though."

She straightened. "Good luck with your new job, Poteet. I mean that. I wouldn't want to see you taking up perfectly good bedspace down at the Perpetual Mission."

" 'Bye, Lucy. Let me know when you want that plastic guy's name. If you say I sent you he'll throw in electrolysis."

Anita was reading *Cosmopolitan* when he came out. He leaned over the desk, grabbed a double handful of her frothy platinum hair, and kissed her square on the mouth. She was still spitting when the glass door gasped shut behind him.

Chapter 11

St. Balthazar Cathedral occupied a city block on Detroit's upper east side, a Gothic dinosaur built with automobile money in 1924. Now it reared four buttressed and gargoyled towers against a backdrop of empty stores, gutted warehouses, and un-finished, never-inhabited, already-decaying HUD houses. The building's surface provided a convenient forum for every local creed whose believers possessed at least a fourth-grade education: peace signs, swastikas, Stars of David, Arabic crescents, laughing Buddhas, devil-worship symbols, and old Yoo-Hoo advertise-ments decorated its brownstone walls outside. Inside, a huge stained-glass window above the doors depicting the Annunciation sported a fresh BB hole through one pane, neatly blacking out the angel's left upper incisor.

The vaulted echoing interior contained four sections of pews with olive-colored runners in the aisles between, a ballustraded balcony circling the base of the cupola, and a twelve-foot crucifix with a bronze Christ writhing in lost-wax agony behind the altar. At His feet, a boy of eleven or twelve dressed in a white robe was busy lighting candles with a Zippo.

○○○○○○

Ralph took the handiest aisle to the altar. He could have made a lot more noise pulling a mechanical duck across Joe Louis Arena.

"Hey, kid." The two words banged around inside the cupola for a while.

The boy went on lighting candles. "You're supposed to uncover your head in God's house."

Ralph took off his hat. "What's your name, kid?"

"Francis Xavier Dillinger."

"Bullshit."

"That's what everyone says."

"Where's your boss, Frankie?"

"Up there on the cross."

"Yeah, yeah. I mean the guy that runs this place."

"Monsignor Breame died. St. Peter came while he slept."

"So did Monsignor Breame. Where's the bishop hang out?"

"The rectory, I guess."

"Where's that, in back?"

"That's where they usually keep it." He was lighting the last bank of candles now. Ralph could feel the heat.

"Ain't you supposed to use one of them long matches for that?"

"They keep blowing out. There's a mean draft in here."

"Show me where the rectory is."

The boy snapped shut the Zippo with an expert flip he hadn't acquired in catechism, genuflected before the big crucifix, and led the way through a door in back onto a flagstone courtyard choked with pigeons.

Ralph was the only man in the Detroit metropolitan area who stepped on pigeons regularly. One of them squawked and fluttered a short distance away, making a neat deposit inside Ralph's hat on takeoff. Cursing, Ralph shook it out and put on the hat.

"You smoke, kid?"

"No sir."

"Drink?"

"No sir."

"Cuss?"

"No, sir!"

"Kid, you need an old man."

The boy pointed out a smaller version of the cathedral surrounded by rosebushes. Ralph left him and pushed the button by the front door. Chimes rang inside. The Bells of St. Balthazar.

When no one answered the second ring, he tried the door. It was locked. He looked back over his shoulder, saw that the altar boy had gone back inside the cathedral, and tried the celluloid window from his wallet. The lock was a deadbolt. Giving up on it, he went around to the back, but his route was cut off by a flower garden surrounded by a six-foot stone wall with a locked iron gate. So much for perpetual church access.

Maybe Bishop Steelcase was snoozing on the couch. The old guy was getting up there, might not remember last night's offer if they didn't discuss it soon. Ralph tried the stained-glass casement window on the side of the little building, then its mate on the other side, which represented either the Three Wise Men on their journey to Bethlehem or the Ritz Brothers. That one was open.

Ralph had never broken into a church. He started counting Commandments on his fingers, but couldn't remember if it was covered. At length he decided rectories didn't count. He hoisted one leg over the casement, then the other.

As he lowered himself into the dim interior, something gave way under his foot. The crash was a lot louder than a mechanical duck. He froze sitting on the casement.

When after a full minute no one had come running from any direction, he supposed the stone walls had swallowed the noise. He lowered himself the rest of the way. Something crunched. He was standing on one of a dozen or more 78-rpm phonograph records.

He wondered about a bishop's taste in music. Kneeling, he read the labels: the theme from *Peer Gynt, The Eroica* symphony, *Perdido, The Magic Flute.* Ralph was standing on Tchaikovsky. There wasn't a Slim Whitman in the collection. He rose with a grunt.

The building was a combination living quarters and office suite, with a narrow entryway meant for hanging hats and coats (the hall tree bore neither), a sitting room with a view of the garden, a small bedroom equipped with a nightstand, reading lamp, and a pointedly diocesan single bed, and two offices, the smaller of which was vacant and was probably the one Ralph would have used had he taken the bishop up on his first job offer. Bishop Steelcase was in none of them.

The larger of the two offices was paneled in dark oak after the masculine priestly fashion and had a big walnut desk with an amber leather top to match the chair behind it. The other chairs in the office were upholstered in tough green Naugahyde and stood on a red Oriental carpet with gold trim, well worn. There were the requisite wooden cross on the wall behind the desk—smaller and much less ancient than the one in the bishop's study—and a case with glass doors, stocked with hardbound and paperback books ranging in subject from the lives of the saints to *The Many Loves of Dobie Gillis.* Ralph reminded himself that the rectory had been used by Monsignor Breame, not the bishop, and that its contents reflected the tastes of the former. (He wondered if the narrow bed had driven the ample prelate to the four-poster in Lyla Dane's apartment.) For all that, this room had an aroma of new tobacco smoke similar to the more established odor that pervaded Steelcase's environment. Well, *someone* would have had to assume leadership of the parish in the pastor's absence.

Ralph inserted his buttocks in the amber leather chair and went through the desk idly. He found the usual drawer stuff along with a dogeared paperback full of Flannery O'Connor's stories about demented Catholics and a Detroit Tigers scorecard.

He wondered what it was about priests and baseball. In the top drawer he came upon a pigskin notepad cover with corners that looked like gold, which he pocketed, pad and all.

That was it. No Frederick's of Hollywood Christmas catalogue, no *Playboy, Penthouse, Gallery, Oui, Screw, Anal Lust, Blue Boy,* or *Balling Bovines,* no X-rated playing cards with fifty-two original and educational positions plus the Joker abusing his orb and scepter in glorious color; not even a medical text with colorplates of the female reproductive system and pop-up clitoris. Either the monsignor had been more cautious than the standard run of closet satyr with desks to hide things in, or someone—Carpenter?—had been through it and confiscated everything incriminating.

Ralph gave the bishop half an hour. Then he gave him forty-five minutes. He read several of the O'Connor stories and understood nothing about them beyond the fact that some authors were a lot bloodier than others. At the end of an hour and a half he used the telephone on the desk to call Steelcase's home. It rang four times.

"This is Philip Steelcase."

"*I'm* here, Your Bishopness," Ralph said. "Where the fuck are you?"

". . . can't come to the phone right now, but if you'll wait for the beep and leave your name and number, I'll return your call."

Shit. Ralph waited, then repeated what he'd said, adding, "This is gonna cost you."

He hung up, realized he'd forgotten to leave his name, and called again. Halfway through the recording someone broke the connection.

Back in the cathedral, Francis Xavier Dillinger had removed his robe to run a Bissell sweeper over the olive-colored runners between the pews. The boy had on jeans, sneakers, and a sweatshirt with Madonna's face on the front and her ass on the back.

"Seen the bishop today, kid?"

"No sir."

"Come in every day, does he?"

"I'm not here every day."

"When you're here, then."

"Usually."

"What time?"

"I don't have a watch."

Jesus, thought Ralph, then glanced self-consciously in the direction of the enormous crucifix behind the altar. "About when?"

"He's always here when I come in at noon and he's still here when I leave after a couple hours." The sweeper went up and down, rattling in the cupola.

"Take a message?"

"I don't have a pencil."

Ralph held out a card. "Tell him I was here. He can reach me at home. He knows the number."

The boy stopped sweeping to put the card in the watch pocket of his jeans. Then he resumed.

"You're with the wrong order, kid," Ralph said. "It's the Benedictines that take the vow of silence."

"Yes sir." He ran the sweeper over Ralph's foot.

On his way home, Ralph sought out puddles with pedestrians standing or walking nearby and ran the Riviera through them. Whenever he splattered one, he celebrated with a swig from his pocket flask; two when he got two with one splash. At a bus stop he scored four senior citizens, a mailman, and a dog relieving itself against an advertising bench and drained the flask. Little victories. If he'd quit his job for nothing, he'd tell Neal English to send the film to both newspapers and all the TV stations and Steelcase could say goodbye to the Vatican over his morning roll and coffee. He stopped at a liquor store to purchase a refill from a counterman who looked like Muammar Khadafy, but after that puddles were hard to find and he had to settle for a bum on Sherman who needed the bath anyway. The bum was wearing a Tyrolean hat just like Ralph's.

Nearing his building, Ralph spotted a tan Chrysler parked in the loading zone and slowed down for a better look. It wasn't unusual for the adult bookstore's customers to wait there for picketers with cameras or passersby who might turn out to be their neighbors to disperse before they went in; but the sidewalks on both sides were deserted, and anyway the Closed sign was still prominent in dead Vinnie's window. Two men were sitting in the front seat. Just as Ralph cruised past, the man at the wheel turned his head and Ralph saw O'Leary's big scorched face and squinched nose framed in the window on the driver's side.

The Riviera's tires bit asphalt, wailed, and threw the car into a two-wheeled turn that dumped over the trash receptacle on the corner. The single wad of Kleenex that was inside stayed there, but as the basket skidded around it swept the orange skins, broken bottles, previously owned condoms, and REELECT THE MAYOR handbills that littered the sidewalk around it out into the street, where the Chrysler, giving chase, lost traction in the wet garbage, spun around, and shattered a taillight against a fire hydrant on the opposite curb. O'Leary backed the car around and started forward again in Ralph's wake. The yelper came on.

Ralph made another right turn, then a left, going through a red light and narrowly missing an eighteen-wheeler trundling across the intersection. The truck braked and swerved, jarring open the doors of its trailer and spilling a shipment of Porta-Potties into the middle of Michigan Avenue. The tan Chrysler careened between the bouncing johns. Ralph cut down an alley and across a disused parking lot with grass growing through cracks in the pavement and found himself heading back the way he'd come minutes earlier, the Chrysler in pursuit.

At that point Ralph remembered the old saying about being nice to people on the way up.

Four angry wet senior citizens waved their canes and shouted obscenities at the red Riviera as it streaked past. A mailman, his uniform plastered with mud, reached into his sack and started throwing packages, some of which burst when they struck Ralph's back window and released a torrent of Civil War chess sets and mail-order toupees. A soaked dog snapped at the Riviera's rear tires.

A very wet bum wearing a Tyrolean hat like Ralph's took a seat on the vacant bus stop bench, drank from a bottle wrapped in a paper sack, and watched the commotion.

Ralph tried for a smuggler's turn at the end of the block. One of his tires hooked the curb and threw the car into a spin. The dog, suddenly finding itself the object of a vehicular chase, ran whining and yipping down the street with its tail between its legs and an orange toupee on its head. Ralph fought the steering wheel as the Riviera struck the curb, bounded off, bumped up and over the one opposite, and came to rest on top of a mailbox with its front wheels spinning.

The sudden stop threw Ralph against the door handle on the driver's side. The door sprang open and he tumbled out onto the sidewalk, catching a glimpse as he fell of the Chrysler stopped in the middle of the street. As he lay on his back, dazed, the dog trotted up, sniffed at him, and lifted its leg.

"Bummer," said the bum.

Chapter 12

"*I* didn't know old people knew them words."

"Words can't hurt you," O'Leary told Ralph. "It's the canes you got to look out for. What'd you do, tell them you were lobbying against Medicare?"

Ralph didn't answer. He was riding in the Chrysler with O'Leary driving. The other man, a uniformed Detroit police officer, had surrendered the shotgun position for the backseat. Ralph was reclining with the back of his head against the head-rest. It still hurt to breathe, but he didn't think he'd cracked or broken any ribs. "What about my car?"

"I called for a tow. I'll give you a chit to spring it from impound. It came off a lot better than the mailbox."

"Don't guess I'll need it where I'm going."

"Ann Arbor?"

"Yeah, yeah. Have your laugh. I didn't croak him."

"Croak who?"

Ralph brought his seat forward. They were on the north-bound John Lodge Freeway, passing the Wonder Bread plant. "Hey, police headquarters is the other way."

"Always has been," O'Leary said. "Just like this always has been the way to Ann Arbor. Well, as soon as we hit the Edsel Ford west."

"What's in Ann Arbor?"

"Later. Who didn't you croak?"

"Who said anything about anybody getting croaked?"

"You did, just now. You said, 'I didn't croak him.' Didn't he?" He glanced over his shoulder at the uniform in the backseat.

"That's what he said, Sarge."

"Don't call me Sarge. You sound like Beetle Bailey. So who got croaked?" he asked Ralph.

"Forget what I said. I'm drunk."

"You smell like it. Drive like it, too. If I was Traffic, I'd bust you. What's the idea of rabbiting when you saw us in front of your place?"

"What was you doing in front of my place?"

"You first."

"I thought you was a process server. I had my fill of them."

"Who hasn't?" O'Leary looped the Chrysler around onto the westbound Ford Freeway. "Step on somebody's toes, did you?"

"The fucking business I'm in is paved with toes. What's in Ann Arbor?"

"You mean the fucking business you *were* in. We stopped in at Lovechild. The lady told us about you getting fired."

"I quit."

"She said different. That woman hates your guts and the box they came in. What'd you do, mistake her office for the men's room?"

"I sent her some albums."

"Jesus, they must have been pretty bad."

"Not if you like yodeling. What's in Ann Arbor?"

"You weren't home, so we knocked on your landlord's

door. He's still out, or maybe he's out again. Did you get to see him last night?"

"No." He said it too quickly. "No, I missed him. Maybe he got lucky."

"Not without a rabbit's foot and the strongest aphrodisiac known to science. He looks just like that bald-headed kid that used to be in the comic strips. What was his name?" O'Leary glanced back at the uniform.

"Don't look here, Sarge. I'm a *Doonesbury* man."

"Don't call me Sarge. Anyway, that's why we waited for you outside, Poteet. I guess you want to know what's in Ann Arbor."

"You read my mind."

"What's in Ann Arbor is the University of Michigan Burn Center. Where they sent Lyla Dane?"

"I remember you telling me."

"She came out of the coma this morning. The docs think she'll make it. Trouble is, she won't talk to any cops."

"Can't think why not. She knows so many."

"Anyway, we need to find out who she made mad enough to try to fricassee her in her own apartment. She's the only one who can tell us, only she won't."

"So why am I going? Oh, shit."

"He's got it," O'Leary told the cop in the backseat, who grunted. "Any idea at all why she wants to talk to you and nobody else?"

Ralph said, "I got a way with broads."

"That explains why you're farting through silk in that penthouse apartment of yours, getting laid every other Tuesday by the wife of a General Motors board member."

"Maybe his member ain't bored," suggested the man in uniform.

O'Leary ignored him. "I don't know what you are to her, Poteet; friend, pimp, favorite john, what, it doesn't matter. She wants to talk to you, which does. We need you to ask her who it was rigged that blast."

"Why the hell should I?"

"Let's just say if whoever it was isn't you, we won't have to bother you anymore about where you were night before last and who you were with."

"That why you brought reinforcements?"

"Excuse my crappy manners. This is Officer Mileaway. Officer Mileaway, this is Ralph Poteet."

"Pleased," said Ralph.

"Yeah." The uniform watched the scenery.

"I brought Officer Mileaway along to remind you what it's like when we bother you."

"I can live with it. Just drop me off at the corner there."

O'Leary drove past it. "Just for the hell of it I ran you through the computer downtown. The information just kept coming out and out. You've spent more time at headquarters than I have. I'm surprised I never saw you there."

"Too much smoke." Ralph opened the window for air. The arson investigator had a cigarette between his fingers and another burning in the ashtray.

"That disturbing-the-peace beef on Livernois last year was a hoot. How'd you get an ordinary camera to work underwater in a Jacuzzi?"

"Saran Wrap. I was proud of them shots. I sent them to *National Geographic* but they bounced them back. I told them they were narwhals."

"Too bad that was his own wife State Senator Coopersmith was with."

"People that age shouldn't be doing that kind of stuff in a public pool."

"I guess it's okay, with a buddy."

Ralph got out a matchstick. "So I had a couple of run-ins with the law. It's the job."

"Bonnie and Clyde had a couple of run-ins with the law. Two more weeks on the premises and you'd qualify for a departmental pension. What I can't figure out is why you aren't rich or dead."

"Luck."

"Which kind, good or bad?"

"It evens out. Am I busted or what? 'Cause if I ain't, this here is kidnapping."

"Technically it's abduction. But that's for private citizens. For a guy with your rap sheet it's an afternoon drive. Relax and enjoy."

Ralph gave up. He had no place to go but home anyway, and if the bishop called, it would do him good to stew a little. Ralph watched the big Uniroyal tire display sliding by and jets taking off and landing at Metro Airport. He had never been on an airplane. He had had a chance once, but arrived late and it left without him, carrying a load of hijacked microchips to Colombia in trade for twelve hundred kilos of high-grade cocaine. On the return trip, a mechanical malfunction had forced the plane down on some jerkwater island in the Gulf of Mexico, where the pilot and copilot were immediately elected to head the revolutionary government. The U.S. State Department was currently considering sending $300 million in military aid to President Ziggy Blumberg and Vice President Oscar Torporino. Ralph had lied to O'Leary about his luck. He always got the short handle.

Inside the Ann Arbor city limits they took the State Street exit and parked in a towaway zone outside the University of Michigan Medical Center. A nurse at the desk in the lobby informed them that the patient had been removed from intensive care and transferred to the third floor of the Burn Center. There a young resident in a white coat with a fresh crop of acne on his chin directed them to a ward at the end of the hall. He hesitated.

"Er, there are rules against that," he said, pointing. "Even if there weren't, don't you think it's, er, inappropriate, considering why these people are here?"

O'Leary apologized and dropped his cigarette butt into a pot containing a rubber tree.

Outside the door to the ward, he showed his badge and ID to a uniformed officer and the three newcomers went in. It was a turquoise room containing four beds, two of them enclosed by curtains. A third was empty, and Lyla Dane lay in the fourth.

Ralph had prepared himself for—what, the Phantom of the Opera? A lot of scars and oozing, anyway. However, except for the white bandages encasing her head like a chain-mail hood and the perennially surprised look of a face with its eyebrows singed off, she appeared to have sustained no frontal damage, for her face was exposed and unmarked. Ralph guessed that she had turned her head at the instant of the explosion. Her arms were swathed in gauze and a tube ran from one to a bottle suspended upside down in a rack beside the bed. Her eyes were closed.

O'Leary bent over her and whispered something Ralph didn't catch. Her eyes opened then and she nodded feebly. Straightening, O'Leary beckoned to Ralph. Ralph shuffled forward reluctantly. He wondered why she had asked for him. What could she have to say to the man who was supposed to have been blown up by the blast she had walked into?

"Nng wu."

He bent down. "What?"

"Ng yu."

"Say again?" He took off his hat and brought his ear very close to her lips.

"Fuck you."

Chapter 13

"*F*uck you?"

"I beg your pardon?" A stern-faced nurse stopped in the act of passing O'Leary to glare at him.

"Talking to a friend." When she'd gone on, he lowered his voice. "Fuck you? That's what she said, fuck you? She had us haul you all this way to say fuck you?"

"I don't think Hallmark has a card for that."

Ralph had told O'Leary the truth because he wasn't sure how much he and Officer Mileaway had overheard. The three were standing in the hallway outside the ward, where the pimple-faced resident had herded them after Lyla Dane had delivered her message and gone to sleep. "Maybe she was delirious," Ralph added.

"I don't think so. I can't figure out this ass-backwards charisma you've got. People go out of their way to tell you what a scuzzbucket you are. How can one man mark up so many enemies before he's sixty?"

"I'm forty-three."

"No kidding? Jesus, what did you do to yourself?"

"Hey, you ain't nobody's Bob Barker neither."

O'Leary lit a cigarette and flipped the match back over his shoulder, narrowly missing Officer Mileaway's left ear. "Back to square one. Where were you night before last?"

"The Vinegaroon on Cass from five to eight-thirty. I got into a chug-a-lug contest with a colored guy named Arvil. Lost by half a mug."

"What was the bet?"

"Loser sprang for the pay toilet."

"No good. You could have gone to Lyla Dane's apartment anytime between eight-thirty and sunup and rigged the switch. Where else?"

"The Macedonian Room from a little after eight-thirty till about ten. A broad belted me with her purse when I followed her into the ladies' room. It was an honest mistake."

"It'd be the first honest thing you ever did. Name?"

"She didn't introduce herself. She had a butterfly tattooed on her ass, if it helps."

"Which cheek?"

"Both of them. It was a big sucker."

"Anyone else who might remember you?"

"Everyone within earshot of the ladies' room."

"What about the bartender?"

"Big guy named Sam. No, wait a minute, that was *Gunsmoke*. They get that all-western channel on cable. I don't remember."

"We'll check the place out. Then where?"

"Florentino's, for about five minutes."

"What can you do in a bar in five minutes?"

"Get tossed out of it by Tino, if you can't pay your tab."

"Next."

"Blind pig on St. Antoine. It's a Christian Science reading room out front. I left there around midnight. They'll remember me. I was the only white raisin in the box. I called Lucille Lovechild at home just before I went out, to settle a bet with a guy named Slade."

"Slade what?"

Ralph shrugged.

O'Leary looked at Mileaway. "We got anyone in the mugs named Slade?"

"They're *all* named Slade."

" 'Kay. Next place."

"Richard's, on John R. Richard remembers me, also a geek named Andy. Buy him a Pepto-Bismol and he'll tell you anything you want to know."

"When'd you leave there?"

"Around one."

"Where'd you go?"

"Straight home."

"So who were the two guys your neighbor Mrs. Gelatto saw you with at four?"

Ralph had a sudden urge—most unfamiliar—to tell the truth. So far he was guilty only of withholding evidence, the kind of charge that got lost in the shuffle whenever the cops cracked a case. Possibly there was a city ordinance against improper disposal of a monsignor; but he could beat that too. Vinnie getting dead made him wonder about how good the photographs he had taken were for insurance purposes. At the same time, the fact that Carpenter (for he was sure it had been no other) had strangled Vinnie while in pursuit of the photographs convinced him of their value. Ralph sighed involuntarily at this near brush with good citizenship.

"I don't remember," he said.

"Holy shit. How come?"

"What do I know how come? I forgot."

O'Leary was one of those cops who scribbled notes on folded sheets of paper. He brushed ashes off his and unfolded to an old section. "Yesterday you didn't even know where you'd been the night before. Today you remember places, times—Christ, even the butterfly on some broad's ass—"

"It might of been a gypsy moth."

"—everything but the names of the two guys who might alibi you out of an attempted-murder beef. Tough break."

"What makes you think old lady Gelatto seen what she says she seen? She's as blind as an elbow."

"Come on, Poteet. What were they, fags? You some kind of Dutch door?"

"Do I look like I swing both ways?"

"No, but neither does my brother-in-law, and he marched on Washington last year. You might've seen him on the news, dotting the second *i* in 'Alternative Lifestyle.'" He snapped his butt at the rubber tree and missed. A little curl of smoke rose from the carpet. "Personally, I don't think you did it. You couldn't change a light bulb without frying your dick."

"Thanks. Sarge."

"Don't call me Sarge."

Ralph put on his hat. "How'd the memorial Mass go? I forgot to ask."

"Too many candles. Those cathedrals are firetraps." O'Leary stepped out of the way of an intern rushing to empty a pitcher of water over the smoldering carpet. "But it was nice, as those things go. My wife says they ought to make a saint out of Monsignor Breame."

"I think somebody already made him."

"What?"

"I said maybe he'll get made one yet," Ralph said.

"Yeah. At the Temple of Lard. After the rosary they'll have to hire a U-Haul to take him to the cemetery. He must've been a tight squeeze in the confession booth." He put away his notes. "Oh, this was on the sidewalk where you fell out of your car. I guess you dropped it."

Ralph stared at the item in O'Leary's hand. It was the notepad from the St. Balthazar rectory, with its gold-and-pigskin cover. "Thanks." He reached for it. O'Leary examined it.

"Pretty fancy. What was it doing in your pocket?"

"Gift from my sister."

"The one in the booby hatch? I thought they made potholders and stuff."

Ralph said nothing. O'Leary gave it to him.

"Sergeant O'Leary?"

The arson investigator turned toward the girl who had called his name. Ralph had seen her out of the corner of his eye—couldn't help it—standing a little apart from a group of interns and nurses at a drinking fountain. She was about Ralph's height and very trim in a bright orange blouse, tan slacks, and high-heeled sandals, a brunette with hair that fell straight down her back to her waist. Her features were fresh and pretty and somehow familiar, although Ralph was certain he had never seen her before. She looked to be about eighteen. When he saw who it was, O'Leary's features softened the way they never would for Ralph.

"Yes, Miss Dane."

"One of the nurses told me Lyla's conscious. Can I talk to her?"

"Maybe later. They just sedated her."

"That makes sense." She pulled a face. Then she saw Ralph. "Hi. I'm April Dane."

"Lyla's sister," O'Leary said. "Say hello to Ralph Poteet, one of your sister's neighbors."

"The private detective. I heard the policemen talking about you before." She held out a slender hand.

Ralph took it. It was cool and dry, unlike his own stubby paw. "Yeah. Uh, I didn't know Lyla had a sister."

"I guess I'm not surprised. I haven't talked to her since I was little. Our parents hung up on her when she called. They're born-again Christians."

"I always wondered how that worked."

"It's kind of like redecorating, only noisier. Right now they think I'm in my poly-sci class. I'm a freshman at Michigan."

"We'd appreciate it if you stayed in touch," O'Leary told her. "Maybe she'll talk to you when she comes around again."

"Probably not. We're strangers. But when you tracked me down as next of kin I had to come."

"Can we give you a lift?"

"My place is just down the street." She turned liquid brown eyes on Ralph. "Mr. Poteet could walk me."

Ralph missed the matchstick he was lifting to his mouth and bit down on his thumb. Officer Mileaway glanced at his superior, who chewed on a cheek.

"Catch a cab?" O'Leary asked Ralph.

"I guess." He sucked his thumb.

Her hair hung straight down as she walked, with Ralph trailing a little behind. Most of the rest of her was in motion. "Listen," he said, "I ain't got much cash on me."

"I could lend you some for the cab. Oh, you think I'm like Lyla."

"Ain't you?"

"No. There's too much disease and stuff out there, and you get arrested. Other than that I think it's a neat way to make a living."

"I guess you ain't born again."

She pulled another face. "God's okay, if you don't make a religion out of it."

"That's what I told my old man, right before he threw the Old Testament at me."

"He quoted from it?"

"No, he really threw it. I had my jaw wired shut for a month."

"Was he born again?"

"Naw. They tried, but there was too many pieces missing." Ralph pressed for the elevator. "He was a preacher."

"I guess we're a couple of Bible brats."

"I guess."

"I bet you had to wear your shirts buttoned to the neck like Beaver Cleaver."

"And a cap."

"No dating till you were sixteen."

"Or after."

"Prayed before every meal?"

"All but the last one."

The bell rang. When the doors opened he held them for her and followed her into the car.

"Are you a real private detective, like Spenser?"

"Spenser ain't real." They started down.

"Well, you know."

"You going to ask to see my gun?"

Her eyebrows went up. They were just a little thick, like Brooke Shields's. "Do you carry one?"

"When I can find it."

"What's your specialty?"

"I take pictures."

"I don't get it."

"Then I won't take yours."

"Oh. You're *that* kind of detective."

"Somebody has to be."

"Do you look for missing persons?"

"When it pays."

The elevator set down. They went out through the lobby. The sun was out, warming the sidewalk. Coeds strolled the sidewalks with their jackets off and no bras.

"What do you charge?"

"Depends on the job. Two hundred a day's the base, expenses extra."

Neither of them said anything for a while. She led him to a Queen Anne house painted gray, with more features than a Swiss Army knife, and he escorted her up three flights of stairs to a tower room with posters of Bruce Springsteen and something called U-2 on the walls. It contained a double bed, a couple of chairs, and a study desk with a gooseneck lamp. A door stood open to a bathroom that made Ralph's cramped one look like an airplane hangar. Kids put up with a lot, he decided. He felt out of place under the ten-foot ceiling in his feathered hat and wash-and-wear suit.

"I want you to find the ones who tried to murder Lyla," April said.

"Uh-huh."

"We weren't very close. But she was—*is* my sister, and even if her life hasn't been so hot, it's hers. Nobody has a right to try and take it. I learned that much from our parents, at least."

"Uh-huh."

"I know the police are trying, but they have a lot of other cases. You were her neighbor. Maybe that means you'll work a little harder."

"Uh-huh."

"Trouble is, I can't afford your rates."

"Uh-*huh*."

"Maybe we could work something out?"

"Uh-uh."

They were standing very close now; the size of the room allowed for little else.

"I'm not my sister," she said, "but I've been around. You know how it is when you get out of a strict home finally." She reached for his fly.

Ralph couldn't remember if he'd put on fresh shorts that morning.

*R*alph's telephone was ringing when he staggered in shortly before two in the morning. With stiffened muscles he lowered himself to the bed and lifted the receiver. "Yeah."

"Ralph?"

"Yeah."

"This is Neal."

"Yeah."

"You okay? You sound like you're a thousand years old."

"What is it, Neal?"

"I been trying to reach you all night. You didn't check in."

"I was busy."

"If you didn't answer this time I was going to send that film to the cops. So did you score?"

"What?"

"The bishop. Christ. Did you make a deal with him for the pictures?"

"I'm working on it." He shifted his weight carefully on the mattress. He felt as if he'd been scrubbed down with a Brillo pad. Which, come to think of it, was not far off. He wondered how the daughter of born-again Christians had learned so many uses for household items.

"Hey, you okay?" Neal asked. "If I didn't know you better I'd swear you been working out."

"Forget it, Neal. I'll check in tomorrow night."

"You better. If you're figuring on cutting me out, I'll have your balls."

"Get in line."

He'd been stretched out fully clothed on the bed for several minutes when the telephone rang again.

"Jesus Christ, Neal."

"Who's Neal?" It was O'Leary's voice.

Ralph groaned. "It's two-fifteen ayem!"

"Thank you. This is the tenth time I've tried to call. I left messages at all the bars you told me about yesterday. You were right about Florentino's. I wouldn't go back there if I were you."

"What's the squeal?"

"Murder, pal. You've been holding out on me."

Vinnie. Ralph sat up, grunting when his sore muscles reacted, and fumbled for his flask. It wasn't in his pocket. "Where are you, downstairs?"

"Hell no. Why should I be downstairs? I'm in Farmington Hills."

"Farmington Hills?"

"Farmington Hills. Is that echo on your end or mine?"

"What's in Farmington Hills?"

"A lot of neurotic dogs with names longer than mine and houses I couldn't afford if I made commissioner tomorrow. And one dead bishop."

"No shit, Steelcase?" Immediately he regretted saying it.

There was a pause on O'Leary's end. "That popped out quick for a Baptist."

Ralph laid the receiver in his lap and mounted an expedition for the pocket flask. It had fallen out of his suitcoat and was wedged between the mattress and his kidneys. There was one swallow in it. Then there wasn't. He wiped his lips on the sheet, then mopped his face.

"Poteet, you there?"

"Yeah. What do I know about a dead bishop?"

"To begin with, you knew his name. I didn't, and my wife's Catholic."

"I'm a trained detective."

Another pause. "I guess you never heard of Dale Carnegie."

"Why call me?"

"Homicide called around to find out who saw him alive last. They got in touch finally with this altar boy named, let's see—"

Ralph tingled.

"Francis Xavier Dillinger," O'Leary went on. "He said His Excellency didn't show up at the rectory today. Somebody else did, though, looking for him. He left his card. You still there?"

Ralph said nothing.

"Yeah, I can hear you breathing. Anyway, nothing's secret downtown, especially not everybody else's cases. Homicide called me. I think you better come down here."

"How come? A card don't mean nothing."

"Because the detective on the case doesn't know you like I do. He's liable to send a couple of uniforms to jump up and down on you until you decide to come. Unconstitutional as all hell, but the Supreme Court's backed up even further than we are. So when can we look for your smiling face?"

By dark, the gray stone house belonged in an old Universal horror movie. Light from the coach lamps threw cruel shadows and the firebushes were an obscene scarlet. Ralph paid his cab-driver, who glanced around at the black-and-whites and un-marked units parked in the cul-de-sac.

" 'Nother B-and-E, I bet," he said. "You couldn't pay me to live in one of these places."

"In that case, let me have my tip back."

The cabbie cranked up his window and tried to run over Ralph's foot.

A uniformed officer let Ralph into the foyer, where the arson investigator greeted him with a pietà tapestry at his back. The Madonna seemed to be squinting against the smoke from his cigarette. "What bus ran over you?" he asked Ralph.

"Long day."

"That a hickey on your neck, or are the mosquitoes running big as roaches this year?"

"I caught it in the cab door. Where's the stiff?"

"In the study." O'Leary didn't move.

"Where's that?"

He grinned. "Yeah, I didn't think you'd fall for that one. This way."

Ralph followed him down the worm-eaten-oak corridor. The door stood open to the study, where a group of uniforms and plainclothesmen stood talking in front of the big desk. One of them was a man half O'Leary's size, with a pinched face and a natty moustache under a narrow-brimmed hat with a silk band. He had on a tight blue suit and looked like a gangster.

"This is Lieutenant Bustard," O'Leary said.

"Any comments?" Bustard had a high sharp voice.

Ralph shrugged.

"Lieutenant Bustard is with Homicide," O'Leary said. "The bishop's behind there."

Ralph took two steps forward and peered over the desk. The white-haired old man lay on his left side on the carpet, wearing the same black cassock Ralph had met him in, or one just like it. Dark blood from the hole between his eyes had made spidery tracks across his forehead into the creamy waves over his left ear. Except for his overturned swivel chair, the room appeared undisturbed.

"Deader'n Jesus," O'Leary said. "We won't have to wait three days."

"There's no need for blasphemy, Sergeant."

"Yes, sir, Lieutenant."

An Oriental man in his thirties sat on his heels beside the body, placing instruments in a black metal case lying open on the carpet. Bustard said, "How long, Doc?"

"Rigor's fully advanced. Six hours, anyway. Maybe longer. Tell me when he had lunch and I'll get back to you." He lifted out a package swaddled in transparent plastic, unwrapped it, and made a face. "Anybody like liverwurst?"

"Angle of entry?"

"Downward, about twenty degrees. No powder burns. Killer stood about ten feet in front of the desk. Maybe if I had some mustard."

Ralph said, "I think I got some on my tie."

"Eighteen feet from the desk to the door," Bustard said. "We measured. Steelcase let him get eight feet inside the room without leaving his seat. That means he was expecting whoever it was." He turned a pair of small pale eyes on Ralph.

"I can't hit a buffalo's ass from ten feet."

"You own a gun?" asked the lieutenant.

"If you want to call it that. I ain't seen it in weeks, though."

Bustard gestured to one of the uniformed officers, who held up a Ziploc bag with a stubby black revolver suspended inside. "This it?"

Ralph started to feel sticky under his clothes. He recognized the new grips. Carpenter hadn't left Ralph's apartment empty-handed after all.

"A gun's a gun," he said.

"I don't blame you." O'Leary tapped ash onto the carpet. "I owned a piece of shit like that, I wouldn't admit it either."

"That been dusted?" Bustard pointed at the telephone on the desk. One of the plainclothesmen said it had. He lifted the receiver and dialed. "We called in the serial number an hour ago. The computer should have kicked out a registration by now."

O'Leary said, "That's two dead priests in two days. You want to tell us anything?"

"You said Monsignor Breame had a heart attack."

"He isn't in the ground yet."

"Great." The Oriental, eating his sandwich on the floor next to the corpse, brushed crumbs off his shirt. "Nothing like going inside an embalmed body forty-eight hours after death to determine cause. Anybody got any salt?"

"Son of a bitch." Bustard slammed down the receiver. "Computer's down."

Ralph said, "I want to report a burglary."

Chapter 15

*T*hey put him in the tank with a hammer murderer, a pair of transvestites accused of stuffing a midget pimp named Chester into an Amana Radarange, and a mountain man awaiting extradition to Idaho to answer charges of abduction, sodomy, and boarding livestock in a neighborhood zoned residential.

The transvestites kept to themselves, and the hammer murderer seemed content to sit on the one available bunk pounding the pillow with the heel of his shoe, but the mountain man developed an immediate affection for Ralph. Since he ran close to seven feet and 500 pounds, with a full black beard that tangled with the hair curling over the vee of his shirt, Ralph was not inclined to discourage his friendship. His name was Warren.

"Ralphie," he said, laying an arm like a tollgate across Ralph's shoulders, "you like sheep?"

"I ain't like them at all," said Ralph with some desperation.

"Bang, bang," said the hammer murderer.

"Didja see his face when I punched 'Cook Code'?" said one of the transvestites.

"No, no," said Warren, putting Ralph into an affectionate hammerlock. "Do you *like* sheep?"

"Well, how do you mean?" Ralph's reply was choked. "Fried in deep fat with mint jelly, or to take out dancing?"

"Bang, bang, *bang!*" said the hammer murderer.

"That wasn't nothing compared to when you stuck the rotisserie up his ass," said the other transvestite.

"Sheep's what we got the most of in Idaho, after potatoes," Warren said. "They serve potatoes with everything out there. If you order fries they give you a baked potato on the side. You can't do nothing with a potato except eat it."

"That's what I heard," said Ralph.

"Sheep, now; they're something else. You ever wrap yourself real tight around a wool blanket on a cold night, Ralphie?"

"Bang, bang, bang, *bang!*" said the hammer murderer.

"We shouldn't of left his keys in his pocket, though," said the first transvestite. "You ain't supposed to put metal in no microwave."

"What you in for, Ralphie?" asked Warren.

"They say I killed a bishop."

"That's bad. A bishop. Wow."

"Tell me about it."

"You should stick to sheep. They almost never die on you. When they do, you can eat them."

"Bang, bang, bang, bang, *bang!*" said the hammer murderer.

Warren was reminiscing aloud about a ewe named Margaret when the guard came. "Poteet."

"Present." Ralph ducked out from under the mountain man's arm and gripped the bars.

The guard shook loose a key from his ring and inserted it in the lock. "You're sprung. Your lawyer's here."

"Which one? I called three."

"Deaf old guy in a green suit. Looks like an abortionist. I think we've had him in here a time or two."

"Oh. Doc Skinner."

"Hey," said one of the transvestites, as the guard was relocking the door behind Ralph. "When do we eat?"

"Hour."

"How come so long? Ain't you got a microwave?" The other transvestite giggled.

"Take care of yourself, Ralphie," said Warren, through the bars. "Don't forget what I said."

"I ain't likely to."

As Ralph accompanied the guard down the corridor, the mountain man took a seat on the bunk next to the man with the shoe.

"Stanley," he said, "you like sheep?"

"Bang, bang, bang, bang, bang, *bang!*" said the hammer murderer.

Lloyd Skinner was waiting for Ralph in the receiving room, along with Sergeant O'Leary, Lieutenant Bustard, and, behind the desk, the same gray-haired Wayne County Sheriff's deputy who had processed Ralph in three hours earlier. The deputy emptied a paper sack full of Ralph's valuables onto the desk and checked them off against a list on a clipboard.

"One silver ashtray."

"Hello, Ralph." Skinner took Ralph's hand in his clammy grasp. He was a shriveled brown man in his seventies, smaller than Bustard, with dirty nails and a hearing aid. He was often mistaken for a disgraced doctor, hence his nickname.

"Hiya, Doc. How's Betty?"

"One crystal toothpick holder."

"You're out of touch, Ralph. Betty was two wives back. It's Fredericka now."

"Wasn't you married to a Fredericka before?"

"No, you're thinking of Henrietta. This one's a cheerleader."

"One notepad in leather cover."

"No kidding, Wayne State?"

"Fordson high. She'll be eighteen in January."

"I thought you looked tired."

"Eleven packages of Sweet 'n' Low."

"What happened to those other two guys I called?" Ralph asked.

"Jack Scavarda's wanted for nonpayment of alimony and Herb Wassermann's in intensive care at Detroit General. He forgot to show up for Fat Phil Camarillo's preliminary hearing last Thursday."

"One gold watch."

"Well, I'm glad *you* showed, Doc. Thanks for busting me loose."

"One silver watch."

"Thank these two. I was just starting to make writ noises when they dropped the charges."

"One watch, metal unknown."

Ralph looked at the two plainclothesmen. O'Leary shrugged and dropped his cigarette butt to the linoleum. "It's the lieutenant's case."

"One rubber gasoline syphon."

"The medical examiner places Steelcase's death somewhere between eleven ayem and two," Bustard said, adjusting his hat. "You were in Lucille Lovechild's office at eleven-thirty, getting fired—"

"I quit."

"—and an altar boy at St. Balthazar says you were at the cathedral from a little before noon until past one-thirty. After that you were in Ann Arbor with Sergeant O'Leary. Now, it's barely possible that you could have killed the bishop in Farmington Hills at eleven and then highballed it downtown in time to—"

"Quit," supplied Ralph.

"—but you'd have needed better luck with the traffic lights than I've ever had, not to mention prowl cars. Except for dressing like my uncle Ed used to, we've got no reason to hold you."

"One zodiac necktie, green," said the deputy behind the desk.

"So can I go?"

"Two matchbooks from Red's Lithuanian Grill and Topless Talent Emporium."

"You could be a good citizen and tell us what your business was with Steelcase," Bustard said.

"Three quarter slugs, two Canadian pennies, and a fifty-cent piece with Art Linkletter's picture on both sides. Sign here."

Ralph signed the receipt and distributed the items among his pockets. "I wanted to give him my condolences on Monsignor Breame punching his ticket."

"You some kind of a magician, mac?" asked the deputy behind the desk.

Bustard took off his hat, ran a finger around the leather sweatband, and put it back on. Except for a neat fringe he was as bald as Vinnie. "Come on, Poteet. He was killed with your gun."

"I said it was stole from my apartment."

"Speak up, Ralph."

Ralph looked at Doc Skinner. "I thought it was your job to tell me not to say anything."

"No, my batteries just gave out." The lawyer took the hearing aid out of his handkerchief pocket and smacked it against a shriveled brown palm.

O'Leary scowled at a fresh burn in his necktie. "I guess we won't be seeing any more of each other, Poteet. Headquarters took the Lyla Dane arson case away and gave it to Lieutenant Bustard."

"Ain't she still alive?"

Bustard said, "Attempted homicide's our beat too. Also there's a connection between what happened to her and what happened to the monsignor and what happened to the bishop: you. You'll talk to me yet."

"In a pig's ass."

"If you prefer. I was going to offer an interrogation room at headquarters."

"Fuck you, Lieutenant."

"Speak up, Ralph," Doc Skinner said.

Ralph snatched the hearing aid out of the lawyer's hand and shouted, "Fuck you!"

"Oh. Don't mention it. I'll send you a bill."

Chapter 16

*I*n the hall leading to the Wayne County Jail exit, Ralph met a bearded man in his twenties wearing torn clothes and struggling with his handcuffs and the two officers who were escorting him toward the cells. The prisoner's eyes were glazed and there was foam in his beard. Ordinarily none of this would have been particularly distressing, but one of the officers was the young man who had spoken with Ralph two mornings before while Ralph was sitting in Carpenter's station wagon next to Monsignor Breame.

Ralph turned toward the wall, ostensibly making room for the grunting trio. As he did so, his gaze locked with the young officer's for an instant. Ralph saw recognition there and then puzzlement as the man sought to place him. Then they were past.

Almost.

Just as they drew abreast of Ralph, the bearded man tore free of his escort's grip. His manacled hands, doubled into a ten-fingered fist, swept up and struck the back of Ralph's head, tilting his hat over his eyes and squashing his face into the cinderblock wall. Ralph saw bright lights and felt a number of capillaries burst inside his nose.

The second officer drew his leaded leather sap from his belt and tapped the raging prisoner behind the left ear. He sagged and the officer caught him.

"Are you all right, sir?" The young officer placed a hand on Ralph's shoulder.

Ralph covered the lower half of his face, bleeding between his fingers, and assumed a high, singsong voice. "Oh yes, Officer, I am being fine, very very fine, thank you."

"You don't look fine, sir."

"Oh yes, I am always looking this way. Very very fine. Thank you, thank you." Bowing maniacally, he backed toward the exit.

"Wait, sir. Haven't we met?"

"Oh no, I would be very very sure if we had met. Very sure. Thank you."

Outside, he leaned back against the door and blew his nose into his handkerchief. He was busy mopping up when a blue 1963 Corvair with a green right-front fender pulled into the curb. Its driver leaned across the seat and rolled down the window on the passenger's side. "Ralph, you okay?"

"Oh yes, I am fine, very very—" He recognized April Dane. His voice came down. "Oh. Hiya. I'm swell."

"Sure? For a minute there you sounded like one of my professors."

"Joke. How'd you find out I was here?"

"When you didn't answer your phone I called Sergeant O'Leary at police headquarters. He said you'd been arrested. For what?"

"It don't matter. They sprung me. Can I get a lift?"

"That's what I'm here for. Where to?"

"My place." He gave her directions.

"O-*kay!*" she said lasciviously.

○○○○○○

He climbed into the passenger's seat. A spring broke and his knees hit his chin. His nose started bleeding again. "Jesus." He fumbled for his handkerchief.

"Sorry about that." She pulled into the street. There was no traffic; the sky was just beginning to lighten in the east. "When I started at Michigan, Lyla wrote me a letter offering to buy me a new Camaro. Our parents found the letter and tore it up. They're still paying on this heap. Everything else goes to the church."

"Uh-huh." He tipped back his head and pressed the wadded handkerchief to his nostrils.

"Last night was nice," she said.

"My hormones are still humming."

She giggled. It sounded better than the transvestites.

"Who taught you that stuff, your sister?"

"No, I didn't talk to her for years, and there was just that one letter. I guess knowing what she did for a living made me curious. You'd be surprised how many boys in high school were willing to help satisfy my curiosity."

"I bet I wouldn't."

"Listen, you don't have any diseases or anything like that, do you?"

"Just my liver."

They rode for a few blocks in silence. The Corvair's tires hissed on the dewy pavement.

"I guess you didn't get a chance to look into what I asked," she said.

"Maybe when you talk to your sister I won't have to."

"Maybe. Sergeant O'Leary thinks you know more about what happened than you're saying."

"That's my building."

"It's a dirty bookstore."

"That's what everybody says. Pull in there."

"The handicapped zone?"

"If they can't wait for this month's copy of *Leather Lovers*, they can damn well send somebody to pick it up for them."

In the foyer she said, "Place needs a good cleaning. Your landlord's supposed to take care of that."

"He's been preoccupied lately." Ralph sniffed surreptitiously as they passed Vinnie's door. No smell yet. He wondered if he should have turned down the thermostat.

Upstairs, April gaped at the door to Ralph's apartment.

"Termites," he said, unlocking it.

She went in ahead of him and stopped in the aisle he'd cleared to his bedroom. When she reached for the light switch, Ralph said, "No!" and placed his hand over it. He took a deep sniff, decided he didn't smell gas, and flipped the switch. "It's a little tricky," he explained.

"My room at home never looked like this. You need a woman."

"What're you, blue cheese?"

"I mean to clean. The place looks like it's been ransacked." She continued to the bedroom and turned on the light. "Wow."

He joined her. "I got out of bed in a hurry."

"It's like one of those murder rooms you see in detective magazines."

"I guess it could use a dusting." He picked up a slashed pillow and stuffed it into a dresser drawer, releasing a cloud of feathers. "Want a drink?"

"What've you got?"

He lifted the blanket on the bed, found a bottle with some liquid in it, and held it up to the light. "Looks like bourbon."

"No thanks." Her tone changed as she turned to face him. "We don't need it."

Ralph's nose started bleeding again.

It was light out when Ralph climbed out of bed onto his hands and knees, pulled himself hand over hand into a standing position with the aid of the bedpost, and dragged himself naked into the cramped bathroom. There he jerked on the light and looked at himself in the mirror over the sink. There was a smear of dried blood on his upper lip—it had stopped oozing finally— and his genitals were plastered to his stomach. They looked depressingly flat. His tongue was pale and his face was tongue-colored. He tried taking his pulse, but couldn't find any spaces between the beats. He drew some water with a clatter of ancient pipes into the smeared glass he kept there and threw it at his face. After a moment he washed himself above and below and crept back into the bedroom.

He stubbed a toe hard against something solid and stuffed a fist into his mouth to avoid crying out. He was deathly afraid of waking April, who was breathing evenly on her back with her eyes closed and the sheet pulled down to expose one white breast. She looked fresh and ready for another round. He felt as if he'd been carrying anvils up and down stairs all night. He wondered if Monsignor Breame had felt the same way, and if this sort of thing ran in the Dane family. The Dane curse. He moaned into his fist.

When the spasm had passed he bent down and picked up the object he'd struck. It was his suitcoat. Carefully he removed the items from its pockets and set them down gently on the telephone stand by the bed, employing the shelf beneath when he ran out of surface. The last was the pigskin-and-gold notepad he'd removed from Bishop Steelcase's desk in the St. Balthazar rectory.

He let the coat drop back to the floor and turned the pad toward the light coming through the window. The top five pages contained names and telephone numbers recorded in the bishop's fine copperplate hand. Ralph recognized the names of several local Catholic Church officials and a number of city politicians and area celebrities, but the rest were unfamiliar. The remaining pages were blank. The third page was too, except for a solitary unidentified telephone number with an area code Ralph couldn't place.

ooooo

April sighed and turned over, displaying a naked length of back.

Quietly, Ralph picked up the telephone, standard and all, and carried it into the bathroom. It barely reached, just allowing him to close the door on the cord. Bracing the standard against the door with his bare belly, he lifted the receiver and dialed the mysterious number.

Waiting for someone to answer, he scratched himself. There was no good reason to stand there with the breeze blowing up his ass, calling someone he didn't know. It wasn't like he was some kind of crusading sleuth who had to get to the bottom of a bishop's murder and the almost-murder of a hooker, regardless of whether the hooker's sister was in his bed. There was no good reason at all, except for the fact that the bishop who had been murdered had been going to pay Ralph's bills for the next decade or so.

"Justice Department."

It was a female receptionist kind of a voice. Ralph said, "The one in Washington?"

"Sir, is there another one?"

"Well, are we talking about the state or the place with the big white buildings?"

"Sir, the state of Washington doesn't have a justice department. It has apples."

"Okay. Let me talk to the cheese."

"Sir, do you mean the attorney general?"

"No lawyers. I want the head honcho."

"Sir, I was referring to United States Attorney General Willard Newton."

Shit. "Well, if you got nobody better."

"What name shall I give him, sir?"

"Just tell him Detroit is calling. Miss?"

"Yes, sir?"

"You got a brother with the Detroit Police Department?"

"No, sir. My brother's with the Washington Redskins. Why do you ask?"

"Just a hunch."

"One moment, sir."

Ralph was placed on hold. After a moment, a raspy, Harvard-leaded voice he recognized vaguely from television news interviews came on the line.

"Carpenter, I told you never to call me here."

Chapter 17

*I*mmediately after Ralph hung up in the most famous face he was ever likely to, April Dane opened the bathroom door, allowing the telephone to drop on his foot. When he was through jumping around, she said, "Important call?"

"Just getting the weather. Jesus." He propped his foot up on the toilet lid and dabbed at the three cut toes with Mercurochrome from the medicine cabinet.

"When I woke up and saw you were gone, I was afraid you'd run out on me. Then I saw the cord and followed it in here." She started to giggle.

"What's funny?" He wiggled the toes. They didn't seem to be broken.

"You are. When you're naked."

He put his foot down and sucked in his stomach. "I don't jog or nothing like that. I got a car."

"I meant the hat."

He looked up at it. "I think I forgot to take it off."

"I couldn't help staring at it. I kept waiting for it to fall off, only it never did."

"Shit."

"What's wrong?"

"I seen your eyes rolling up. I thought it was for another reason."

She grasped him by the most available handle and drew him near. She was naked too. Her dark hair was tousled and her face looked fresh without makeup. He could feel the heat from her body, or maybe it was from his. Every part of him protested except the part she was holding.

"It wasn't *just* the hat," she said.

"No?"

"Uh-uh. Come back to bed."

"I got work to do."

"You can't start work until I finish paying your retainer."

"I think I owe you change now."

"Well, pay up." She gave him a squeeze.

"What about your sister?"

"Let her find her own detective. You're my private dick, right?"

"Uh-huh." He gritted his teeth.

"Hardboiled dick."

"Jesus."

"The heat." She applied a hydraulic motion.

"Damn."

She looked down at him. "Whoops."

He let out his stomach then. There wasn't much point in holding it in any longer.

"Go away, Ralph."

Neal English was seated in a semicircular booth upholstered in red leather in the Cadillac Club on West Lafayette, under a framed caricature of Herve Villechaize. The insurance actuary's monolithic face, ripe for a caricature of its own, was framed by a white bib with a scarlet lobster on it. The remains of a similar life form lay on his plate, where he was busy dismantling it with a mallet. Ferns decorated the room, swaying to classical music turned down very low.

"The girl in your office said I'd find you here." Ralph slid into the booth.

"Next time you talk to her, tell her she's fired."

"You get anything out of them big cockroaches, or do you just like to wrestle?"

"I see nobody killed you yet." Neal crushed the lobster's skull and picked out its brains with a miniature fork.

"That's why I'm here."

"I'll do you after this lobster."

"You always was a card, Neal." Ralph returned his menu to the waiter, a plump man with white hair and a red face. "Ain't you got no burgers?"

"The ground sirloin is quite good, sir."

"Okay, burn one and slap on a slice of Velveeta. None of that Swiss crap."

"Would you like a beverage?"

"What's on tap?"

"We have a full assortment of imported beers."

"That Mexican piss gives me the trots. Bring me a Blatz in a can. I found a rat hair in a bottle once," he confided to Neal. "What're you waiting for, Maurice, your tip?"

"May I take your hat, sir?"

"Why, your head cold?" When the waiter had withdrawn, Ralph winked at Neal. "What do you think, he does it to the busboy or the busboy does it to him?"

"Jesus Christ, Ralph."

"They're the only people that can carry a tray without dropping it. It's all in the hips." He took a gulp of Neal's ice water. "Listen, you still a whiz with computers?"

"I never was to begin with."

"Sure you were. I seen you put Arnie on line when we was with Great Lakes."

"I helped him set his digital watch."

"You got a computer where you are now?"

"I'm on timeshare, with an office-system Kaypro."

"No shit? Congratulations. What I want to know is, you got a computer where you are now?"

Neal broke the lobster's neck. "Why?"

"I want to bust into the computer files at the Justice Department."

"Okay, don't tell me. I wasn't going to do anything for you anyway."

"No, I mean it."

"You're talking about the Justice Department in Washington, D.C.?"

"They don't have one in the state of Washington. I asked."

"What is it you want to find out?"

"Why Willard Newton would want to kill a prostitute and a bishop, and what that has to do with a dead monsignor."

"Willard Newton."

"That's the man."

"The secretary of state?"

"No, the attorney general."

"That's Gregory Tobin."

"I think Gregory Tobin's Health, Education, and Welfare," Ralph said.

"No, that's Henry Wazuki."

"Henry Wazuki's the place kicker for the Miami Dolphins."

"*Their* files I can break into."

Ralph's ground sirloin came, on a big plate with broccoli, parsley, and less identifiable pale, rounded vegetables arranged artfully around it.

"This joint running low on produce?" he asked the waiter. "I could drive a truck between the carrots and onions."

"Those aren't onions, sir. They're leeks."

"Don't say it," Neal warned.

"Am I supposed to eat this shit or frame it?"

"Sir, you may shove it up your ass for all I care." The waiter left.

"Don't tip him," Ralph told Neal. "He forgot my beer."

"What makes you think the attorney general would want to kill anyone?"

"When I called this number I found in Bishop Steelcase's notebook and told the broad it was Detroit calling, Newton came on and called me Carpenter." Ralph spoke through a mouthful of ground sirloin. "Carpenter's the one booby-trapped the hooker's apartment. You'll hear about the bishop on tonight's news."

"It was on the radio this morning. Cops have a suspect in custody."

"That was me. They kicked me at sunup. So what about the computer?"

"Those things have security codes. I couldn't get in if I wanted to."

"Sure you could. Just last week I read where some kid in Jersey tapped into the Pentagon and sent four hundred cases of Trojans to Tehran."

"A worthy cause, if it cuts down on the number of little Iranians," Neal said. "So get the kid."

"This ain't a favor, it's a business proposition. When they took down the bishop, the meal ticket went with him. Before that we stood to split a thousand a month for life." He cut the figure in half out of habit. "If Steelcase was going to pay that much to hush up what happened to the monsignor, think what Newton would contribute. All them jerks in Washington want to be president."

"Why would Newton care how a Detroit priest died?"

"That's what I want to find out. It's hard to blackmail somebody when you don't know what you got on him."

"I've got a better idea. Why don't I just give you back your pictures? I'm not cut out to be a crook. I stink at it."

○○○○○○

"There could be a million in it."

"Dollars?"

"Hell, BMWs. You ever seen what a politician pays the phone company?"

Neal pushed away his plate. "I'd need to program the machine to keep throwing codes until it accessed."

"Sure. Whatever."

"You didn't let me finish. I can't do that on my system. You need an office computer for that."

Ralph chewed and thought. "If I get you one, can you do it?"

"You don't find them in the five-and-dime. You need the use of a state-of-the-art system for several hours."

"Answer the question."

Neal sighed. "I was honest before you came along. Yeah, I can do it."

"I knew it. From now on it's you and me, pal, fifty-fifty. Just like the old days."

Neal glared at him from under his heavy brows. "You cross me, I'll have your balls for breakfast. I've got a client owes me a favor. G. Gordon Liddy fired him because he scared him."

"I never stiff friends." Ralph finished his meal and rose. "Don't forget what I said about the tip."

Chapter 18

"*A*nita, call security," Lucille Lovechild said into the intercom. "It's back."

Ralph, standing in front of her desk holding his hat, said, "I ain't here to cause trouble. I changed my mind about that severance pay."

"Cancel security, Anita."

"Phooey," the receptionist's voice crackled. "Get me all excited, then quit. Just like my first husband."

Lucille sat back, toying with her eyeglasses. She had on a blue suit with a skinny necktie that made her look like Nixon. "What happened to your new job?"

"Small delay. The boss died."

"My condolences. Was it before or after he sobered up and found out whom he'd hired?"

"The offer's still good. I just need operating expenses till it comes through. I just paid forty to get my car out of the impound."

"How much were we paying you?"

"Three hundred a week."

"Try one-sixty. Of which we withheld fifteen." She pressed

the intercom button. "Anita, cut Poteet a check for two hundred and ninety dollars."

"What'd he do, sell you his entire wardrobe?"

"Just make out the check."

While they were waiting, Ralph put on his hat. "How're things in the hole?"

"If you mean the file room, I'm turning it into an employee lounge. Everything's in the computer and I don't need a place to hide you anymore."

"What'd you say?"

She raised her eyebrows. "I don't need a place to hide you anymore?"

"No, before that."

"The files are all in the computer. Why?"

He shrugged elaborately. "Uh, what's Chuck Waverly up to?"

"Forget Chuck Waverly. He doesn't exist for you. I have hopes of turning that young man into a first-class operative and the last thing he needs is to keep company with a dime detective like you." She said it with some heat.

Ralph got out a matchstick. "I was right about Klugman, huh? He was tapping his own till for some skirt."

"I don't discuss this firm's cases with outsiders. Thank you, Anita."

The platinum-haired receptionist handed Lucille the check and slapped Ralph. The noise was like a pistol shot.

He put a hand to his cheek. "You had some lint on the back of your dress."

She slammed the door behind her.

Lucille signed the check and held it out. "Take care of yourself, Poteet. It's a cinch no one else will."

"Babies get took care of. Grownups need cash." He folded the check and put it in his breast pocket.

"That's your exit line."

In the reception room he hesitated. The Rolodex containing the home addresses and telephone numbers of personnel, Chuck Waverly's included, was in plain sight at Anita's left elbow. She was reading a magazine as usual.

"Anita, you got a smudge on your nose."

"Ralph, I got a pain in my ass." She didn't look up.

"No, I mean it. You better go powder it or whatever it is you broads do."

"I'll powder my nose when the pain in my ass is gone."

Ralph, deep in thought, was getting into his car in the parking lot when a brand-new yellow Volkswagen Rabbit pulled into the space next to his.

"Mr. Poteet?"

"Go fuck yourself." He slammed his door. Then he opened it again. "Kid, is that you?"

Chuck Waverly was beaming over the Volkswagen's roof. His hair was fiery red in the afternoon sunlight, putting the carrots in the Cadillac Club to shame. "Hello, Mr. Poteet. I was afraid I wouldn't see you again."

"How was jail, kid?"

"Worse than I expected. You wouldn't believe what they put me in with."

"If it wasn't a mountain man named Warren, you was ahead of the game."

"I wanted to thank you for that advice. Klugman was in the room next door when the excitement broke out at the Acre of Ecstasy. It made him nervous and he dropped his insurance claim. Mrs. Lovechild gave me a bonus."

"I bet she loved that."

"She acted like I was holding her up. But she made up the bonus rule, so she couldn't refuse. She also put a reprimand in my file for violating company policy."

"Forget about it. If reprimands was bullets I'd be a tennis racquet."

OOOOOO

"I wasn't complaining. I made a down payment on this car with the bonus."

Ralph sensed something. "You got your priorities in order, kid. Glad I could help." He started the Riviera. As he was turning his head to back out of the space, he locked gazes with Waverly, who was standing by the Riviera now and bending down. Feigning surprise, Ralph cranked down the window. "What now, kid?"

"I was just wondering."

"No good. Hurts the head. Spit it out."

"I was thinking, maybe if you weren't too busy sometime, I could tag along with you on a case and get some pointers. You know, about detective work."

"What case? I'm unemployed."

"Not for long, I bet."

"Forget it, kid. It's the jail food talking. That saltpeter does something to both ends."

"The best detectives always went to jail. Lew Archer—"

"A wienie. They'd bugger him into next Tuesday at County. Anyway, he wasn't real."

"I know that. I just thought—"

"I don't know, kid." Ralph chewed his matchstick. "I might be working on something you can help with."

"Great! What is it?"

"Hang on. It'd be like an internship. No pay, just experience."

"What do you want me to do?"

Ralph smiled. "You got access to that computer Lucille's always bragging about?"

Ralph's apartment still smelled of April Dane. He couldn't tell if it was a scent she used or if it was just her, but it lingered hours after she had caught a cab home to Ann Arbor. He opened a window to let in some of the mildewy Detroit air he was used to and called Neal's office.

"Go away, Ralph."

"How'd you know it was me?"

"Because I'm busy."

"Listen, we're meeting Chuck Waverly at Lovechild Confidential Inquiries tonight at ten."

"What's a Chuck Waverly?"

"Young squirt at Lovechild thinks I spit the moon. I didn't tell him what we needed to find out, just said we needed to break a security code. He says the office machine can handle it. He's letting us in after closing."

"What'd you promise him?"

"Hands-on training from the best private star in Detroit."

"The guy on West Grand River?"

"Funny. Can you make it?"

"I guess so. Do I need a black turtleneck and one of those two-foot-long flashlights?"

"Not to go in the front door. This is strictly legal, I tell you."

"Boss know about it?"

"That'd just complicate things."

"So we're breaking in."

"Hell no," Ralph protested. "The kid's got a key. Just to be safe, though, we're going in the back door. The cops might not know we got a right to be there."

"Uh-huh. You said ten o'clock?"

"Ten, like in ten times a thousand makes a million."

"More like ten to life. I'll be there." Neal hung up.

Ralph spent the next half hour tidying the apartment. He straightened overturned chairs and tables, threw his shirts and underwear into their proper drawers, replaced cushions with the slashed sides down. When he was through with that, all the place needed was a mop and a bucket of disinfectant, like always. Finally he emptied the dregs of three different kinds of liquor from six bottles into a glass tumbler and emptied that down his throat. He dumped the empties into a plastic garbage bag with the rest of the debris, opened the bedroom window, took aim on the dumpster in the alley, and let go. It landed with a *whump*, displacing a similar amount of senior trash and sending two cats and a man in a dirty sports jacket and a hat like Ralph's over the side. Then he went downstairs. The dregs had only whetted his thirst.

" 'Afternoon, Mrs. Gelatto," he said as he rounded the second-floor landing.

The old woman standing at the foot of the stairs looked up, adjusted her thick glasses, and pointed a red-knuckled finger. "That's him!"

Then Ralph saw the young police officer standing next to her, the one he'd seen twice before. In front of them the door hung open to the apartment where Ralph had stashed Vinnie's body. The officer unholstered his revolver.

"Freeze!"

Ralph had never heard a policeman actually say it before, except on television, which was where he suspected the officer had got it. He wondered if anyone ever froze. His instincts told him not to. He had turned and now was running up the stairs he'd just come down. Behind him he heard other feet pounding.

On his floor, panting, he fumbled for his keys, then said to hell with it and went through what was left of the door, which started his nose bleeding again. The window where he'd stood to dump the trash was still open. Without hesitating he ran to it, let himself over the sill, sat there for a second, then, as footsteps hit the hallway outside his apartment, pushed off. For a second he was airborne. Then, with a jolt that drove his knees into his chin, he was sitting among the coffee grounds, banana skins, squashed Dixie cups, and five of the six very hard liquor bottles he had thrown out moments before.

When he pushed his hat back from his eyes, his face was inches from that of the man in the Tyrolean and dirty jacket, who had evidently just returned to the dumpster. He had the sixth bottle tipped upside down and was rubbing at the inside of the neck with a crusty finger. Ralph recognized him as the bum he had splashed yesterday.

The man sucked on the finger and screwed up his face. "You *drink* this shit?" he said.

Chapter 19

*R*alph couldn't believe his luck. Although black, the derelict was built along his own slightly dumpy lines and their hats were the same except that the feather was missing from the derelict's and the nap had worn off, leaving it shiny in spots. The only jarring note was the sports jacket, orange-and-green plaid under a patina of filth. Ralph's suitcoat was a more conservative dark polyester.

"You got roller skates or what?" Ralph asked. "I thought all you bums stayed in one place."

"I ain't no bum," said the bum.

"What are you, Miss October?"

"When them Christmas decorations go up in Hudson's, I'm one of the homeless."

"Can you drive a car, Homeless?"

"Is Carlos king of Spain?"

"That mean you can drive a car?"

"Hey, I wasn't always like this. I was Jimmy Hoffa's bodyguard."

"Homeless, how'd you like to make ten bucks easy?"

"Did Gabriel García Márquez win the Nobel Prize?"

"Let me guess. You sleep in the library."

"Man, you can find me between Hispanic Studies and Istanbul any Tuesday. That's the tall-books shelf; I toss around some," he added, smiling with three teeth that had never been introduced.

Ralph held up a ten-dollar bill. "First, we change jackets."

Homeless frowned speculatively, put down the empty bottle, and felt one of Ralph's lapels between thumb and forefinger. "I'm partial to wool," he said. "But okay."

They made the exchange. Ralph handed him the bill and his keys. "There's a red Riviera parked in front of the building. Get to it and scratch rubber. You'll be chased."

"Cops or Mafia?"

"Cops."

"Okay. I don't mess around with no Cosa Nostra. Where you want me to leave it?"

"Ditch it anywhere. It ain't mine and the owner's got other problems." Ralph heard running footsteps in the alley. "Get going."

"They be shooting?"

"That shouldn't bother Jimmy Hoffa's bodyguard."

"Back then I wasn't standing in front of no bullets for less'n twelve yards a week."

"What can I say? The market's thin."

Homeless shrugged, squared his hatbrim, flicked an orange peel off the sleeve of Ralph's suitcoat, and vaulted over the top of the dumpster. Ralph heard the officer shout "Freeze!" again and then there were galloping footsteps. A shot made the sides of the dumpster ring. Under the echo he heard more running, probably the officer's.

He stayed where he was even after he heard the Riviera coming to life with the terrible grinding noise of a tortured starter and then the shrilling of rubber on asphalt, indicating that Homeless had made his escape; he wasn't sure whether the officer had called for a backup to watch the alley. He spent the time among the wet coffee grounds and used Kleenexes deep in a philosophical study. This wasn't the cushy spot he had been anticipating.

After about ten minutes he grasped the edge of the dumpster and peered over. One of the slat-sided cats he had frightened away earlier was licking an empty plastic meat tray on the pavement. Otherwise Ralph appeared to be alone. He climbed out. The loud jacket had begun to itch ominously.

Just to be sure he wasn't seen, he scaled the alley fence into the parking lot next door, stepped out into a side street, and walked for several blocks along the sides of buildings not intended for public viewing. The air had become chill and he took his warmth from the legality of his condition and the exhaust fans blowing kitchen odors from Thai restaurants, bar grills, and diners run by men named Mac and Buster with their service records tattooed on their forearms. At length he came out on Michigan Avenue, where six cabs passed him by before a nearsighted, born-again Christian hack driving an old Checker took pity on the man in derelict's clothing and stopped.

"Let's see your cash, brother."

Ralph got his wallet out of his hip pocket and showed him. The driver peered at the picture of the costar of *The Dukes of Hazzard.*

"Okay, hop in, Mr. Wopat."

In the cab, Ralph felt something in the right side pocket of his jacket, found a half-eaten Ding Dong that had either been thrown into the dumpster or belonged to Homeless or both, sniffed at it—he hadn't eaten since the Cadillac Club—and reluctantly tossed it out the window when it proved to be moldy. He caught the driver glaring at him in the rearview mirror.

"Where to, Tom?"

Ralph hesitated. He had five hours to kill in a city that was hunting him for murder. "Ann Arbor," he said. "I'll tell you where to go when we get there."

"Folks generally do, brother."

The trip was memorable. The driver provided Ralph with a detailed account of how he had come to find Jesus and, somehow avoiding blasphemies, managed to curse at every driver who changed lanes within his vision, which extended roughly eleven inches beyond the Checker's hood. It was like being driven by a Mrs. Gelatto with religion. In Ann Arbor, they shot across an intersection a full ten seconds after the light had turned red, with a city police car just two cars behind them. Through the back window Ralph saw its flashers come on, but then the cab roared over a steep hill and swung around a corner at the bottom, bumping over the curb and scattering a group of young men dressed in fraternity sweaters waiting to cross the street.

"I think you lost him," Ralph said.

"Lost who, brother?"

"Jesus Christ."

"Yes, brother, yes."

Three major traffic infractions later and two blocks from April Dane's apartment, Ralph told the driver to pull over and got out.

The driver took his fare. "Good luck to you, Mr. Wopat. I know you'll see the light."

"It's a wonder *you* did."

April opened her door wearing a Bruce Springsteen sweatshirt and cutoffs. Her feet were bare and her hair was tied behind her neck. When she recognized Ralph, her face brightened. "Hi!"

"Yeah. Lemme in. There's a campus cop downstairs."

She stood aside and he swept past her. "Are you in some kind of trouble?" She closed and locked the door.

"Same old kind. You got anything to drink?"

"Just Diet Coke."

"You're kidding."

"I don't drink. I could go get something."

"Better not. Might make someone suspicious." Standing to one side of the window, he peered out between the curtains.

"Ralph, what's wrong?"

"To begin with, wieners come in packages of ten and you can only get eight buns to the bag."

"So?"

"So no matter what you do you wind up with either two extra wienies or six extra buns. There ain't no way around it and the rest of life's just like it."

"I can fix you something if you're hungry."

"Naw, the Ding Dong spoiled my appetite."

"Could you repeat that? I just got back from class and my head's still full of Abnormal Psychology."

"Mine too. What time is it? I got coffee grounds in my watch."

"A little after six."

He turned on her portable TV set. The news was full of election campaigns and other natural disasters. "This just in," said the announcer.

"Ralph?"

"Sh."

"The owner of an adult bookstore downtown was discovered dead in his apartment an hour ago, the victim of an apparent strangling. Vincenzo Capablanca, age fifty-one . . ."

April stared at the live footage of Ralph's building. "Isn't that—?"

"Shut up."

". . . a tenant, who summoned the police. Police pursued a suspect from the building, who escaped in a late-model red Buick Riviera. . . ."

"Ralph!"

". . . suspect's name has not yet been released. We will return after this with an update on that scandal involving Democratic State Senator Grover Greene and the Clawson girls' curling team." The announcer's face dissolved to a close-up of Ed

McMahon holding a package of Little Soldier condoms. Ralph turned off the set.

"You didn't do it, did you?" April asked.

"I ain't been to Clawson in months."

"You know what I mean."

"Some geek named Carpenter did him in my apartment. The old lady from upstairs seen me moving the body."

"Today?"

"Couple of days back. It just never come up in conversation."

"Does this have anything to do with my sister?"

"Did you talk to her?"

"No. Every time I'm there she's under sedation. It *does* have something to do with her."

Ralph scratched under his left arm. "Listen, you wouldn't happen to have a can of Black Flag in the house."

"No. Answer me."

"Lysol might do it."

"Ralph!"

He shrugged. "Yeah. This monsignor bought the farm in your sister's bed. I got rid of the body for her and now this Carpenter guy that works for the bishop wants to do me. Your sister and my landlord just got in his way."

"How long have you known?"

"Since I found out that what happened to your sister wasn't no accident. Burn this, okay?" He took off the jacket and held it out.

She didn't take it. "You knew all along and you didn't say anything."

"It was too complicated. Listen, I'd burn it myself, only I can't go out."

"What are you doing, blackmailing the bishop?"

"Me? Hell no." She was quicker than he'd expected.

She unlocked the door and flung it open. "Get out of here."

"I can't."

"I'll yell rape."

"I was going to yell that last night, only I didn't have enough wind."

"Rape!"

"If I go out, they'll nab me for Vinnie's murder."

"Rape!"

"When O'Leary and Lieutenant Bustard find out, they'll hang Lyla on me too."

She took a deep breath.

"Okay, okay!" he said quickly. "I was knocking a little off, who wouldn't? Now the bishop's dead too. I'm pretty sure I know who sicced Carpenter on him and Vinnie and Lyla, but I don't know why. I can't find out till tonight, which is why I got to hide out here."

The campus officer Ralph had seen downstairs came to the door with his revolver in his hand. He had gray hair and a beer belly and a face like a doubled fist. "Who hollered rape?"

"Me," Ralph said.

The officer covered him. "This guy try something, miss?"

"April—"

"Be quiet, you! What about it, miss? We'll put this guy in County with Big Cecil Norden. He ain't had a woman in two years."

"You ought to introduce him to this guy Warren in the Wayne lockup."

"Shut up, you! Miss?"

She hesitated, then shook her head. "Nobody yelled rape here."

"You sure? He looks like a prevort to me."

"You ain't no Broderick Crawford yourself, Jack."

"I'm sure. Thanks for checking it out, Officer."

"No problem." He put away the weapon. "Sorry about that, bub. We get some maggots here sometimes."

"You'll know what to do with this, then." Ralph held out the jacket.

The officer left without taking it. To April, Ralph said, "That mean I get to stay till tonight?"

"I want to find out who hurt my sister."

"I'll keep you posted."

"You've got the post for it." She smiled.

Uh-oh, thought Ralph.

She took the jacket from him, opened the window, and hurled it out. Then she plucked off his hat and threw it after the jacket.

"Hey!"

"Rape," she whispered.

On the sidewalk in front of the house, a scraggly-bearded man in patched trousers and a pair of dark glasses held together with a Band-Aid set down his scuffed cello case, picked up the jacket, looked it over, and put it on. Then he retrieved the cello case and strolled away, scratching himself and leaving the hat where it had landed. It was still there when Ralph came staggering out three hours later.

Chapter 20

*T*he driver Ralph drew on his way back to Detroit wasn't a born-again Christian or any other kind, judging by the fact that the name on his license was Muhammed Daktari. The radio station he listened to played nothing but reggae, which had Ralph's head beating in counterpoint by the time they reached Romulus. An updated news report identified Ralph by name as the suspect wanted for questioning in the murder of Vincenzo Capablanca and provided a description that depressed him deeply. Fortunately, he had had the presence of mind to keep his face in shadow from the moment he got into the cab.

He got out three blocks away from Lovechild Confidential Inquiries, tipped more than his customary quarter so that the driver wouldn't have reason to remember him, and walked the rest of the way. It was a bitterly cold night, one of those glaciers-approaching evenings that Michigan gets halfway between the sopping heat of August and the sterile polar blasts of January, and it caught Ralph in his shirtsleeves. Even worse, he lengthened his journey by crossing the street whenever another pedestrian appeared on his side. Once a police cruiser turned into his block and he ducked behind a hedge on the front lawn of a funeral home, not ten minutes after somebody's dog had made a stop on the same spot. When he resumed walking, his nose was running and he stank to heaven, and it wasn't even Saturday night.

"Ralph!"

The name rang off the walls of the shallow portal to the Lovechild offices. Ralph was halfway down the block, running hard, when he realized it was Neal English who had called to him. He reversed directions and climbed the steps to the door a second time. Neal was huddled in the shadows of the entryway, hands in the pockets of a light topcoat with a fur collar. He looked like a statue of Lincoln.

"Man, you got guts. They got the bloodhounds out looking for you."

"I think I just missed one." Ralph scraped his heel on the edge of the top step.

"So did you do it?"

"Hell no. It was somebody's mutt."

"I mean your landlord. Couldn't you make the rent this month?"

"That was Carpenter."

"This the same Carpenter did the bishop and tried to do the hooker?"

"Ain't one of him enough?"

"What's he got, a bad case of piles?"

"He whacked Vinnie on account of Vinnie and Carpenter both showed up in my apartment at the same time looking for the film. I think he whacked Steelcase because Steelcase was fixing to buy me off. I figure he's running his own game, or else he's in with Willard Newton."

"The secretary of state?"

"The attorney general. Jesus Christ."

"The guy on the news said a witness saw you with Vinnie the last time anyone saw him."

"That was Mrs. Gelatto. She's blind as a boot. Vinnie was already dead then. I was moving him from my place to his."

"That's two bodies in one week. You in training for the coroner's office?"

Ralph stamped his feet. "Where the hell is Waverly with that key? We're tripping over brass monkey balls out here."

"You're too hot to be cold. I think you just set a new record for deep shit."

Chuck Waverly joined them moments later. The young operative's red hair was touseled and the cold had reddened his cheeks. He looked just like Howdy Doody.

"Mr. Poteet! I wasn't sure you'd show up. Did you know the police are looking for you?"

"It was Carpenter."

"Who's Carpenter?"

Neal said, "Carpenter's the one did the bishop and tried to do the hooker."

"What hooker?"

"All I know is it's got something to do with Willard Newton."

"The ambassador to Norway?"

"Jesus Christ," Ralph said. "Open the fucking door. My ass has got icicles."

Waverly produced a key and unlocked the glass door, then threw an arm in front of Ralph when he started inside. "I've got to disarm the burglar alarm."

Ralph watched him press a sequence of buttons on a keypad on the wall inside the door. "I didn't know the place had a burglar alarm."

"Mrs. Lovechild had it installed right after she fired you."

"I quit."

"We can go in now."

Ralph and Neal accompanied Waverly through the deserted reception area and down one of the pastel corridors. When the young man reached for a wall switch, Ralph stopped him.

○○○○○○

"It's all right," Waverly said. "I have clearance to come in after hours. It isn't like we're breaking in."

Neal peered at Ralph through the gloom. "Is he putting us on?"

"The only thing Chuck ever put on was his shorts; the kind with little teddy bears on them. Come on, kid." He put an arm across Waverly's shoulders. "Let's you and me and Neal go shoot some clams."

The computer room was lined with dials and rows of colored panels, with a lagoonlike space in the center where one person could sit comfortably at a console with a screen and a keyboard. Neal swept past Waverly as the young man was explaining the system, claimed the seat, and began working the keyboard like Lon Chaney at the organ. The rapid clacking of his fingers striking the keys reminded Ralph of the set of battery-operated teeth he had given his wife for their third anniversary.

"Entry code," Neal demanded.

"Watson." Bathed in the green glow of the screen, Waverly's face was little-boyish.

Neal tapped out the password. The screen flashed instructions Ralph couldn't read. Neal's fingers hesitated only briefly, then flew over the board.

"Security access."

"Marple."

More clacking. The letters on the screen looked like little bugs to Ralph; but then his good eye wasn't much better than the glass one at night.

"Secondary security access. Jesus."

"Spade," Waverly said.

Neal paused. "Who programmed this system?"

"Mrs. Lovechild."

"I'm starting to see why she chose this line of work."

Ralph said, "She even looks a little like Bulldog Drummond."

"Speaking of dogs, did one take a dump in here?"

Ralph looked down at his shoes. "Hell, I bet I left a trail of shit all the way."

"Why should tonight be different from any other time?" Neal entered the code. "Okay, boys and girls, we've got the full power of six miles of electronic pasta behind us. Now we're going to try and break into the Justice Department files. If we're in luck, the security code on their end will have something to do with Willard Newton, the Justice Department, or the attorney general's office. If we're not, some junior clerk programmed the street address of the first girl he ever fucked and we can be sitting here running possibilities from now until the next time the Tigers win the World Series. Start spitballing."

"We don't have to," Waverly said. "The system has a decoding system and memory banks full of current events updated to the first of this month. Enter any one of the three headings you mentioned and it will run all the combinations quicker than you could read them."

Neal whistled. "What'd your boss do, hit the lottery?"

"She's running an account. I figure she'll have it paid off about the time someone donates the system to the Smithsonian."

"Beats the hell out of my Kaypro."

"Kaypro's overrated. You can get all of this year's features on last year's Apple and eat for a week at the London Chop House on the difference."

"Fellas?" Ralph said.

"I had an Apple. That's why I went to Kaypro."

"You must've got a bad one. I'm coming up on three years on mine without a service call."

"Fellas?"

"I had nothing but," Neal said. "One time a cloud passed in front of the sun and I lost thirty pages of actuaries into the stratosphere."

"You must've done something wrong. I bet you hit the Delete key by accident."

"I didn't even have my hands on the keyboard."

Ralph placed two fingers in his mouth and blew. The whistle that resulted wasn't as shrill as he'd hoped, but the other two stopped arguing and looked at him.

"This shit is fascinating, I mean, really," Ralph said. "Hey, I got a hard-on just listening. But right now some guy in Washington's sitting on his fat butt behind a big desk drawing steaks and chops on my picture, and you can jam your Kaypro up your Apple for all I care whose is bigger. Can we get back to work?"

"There isn't a steak or a chop on you, Ralph. You're all rump roast. Here goes." Neal entered WILLARD NEWTON, U.S. ATTORNEY GENERAL, and JUSTICE DEPARTMENT, then sat back and folded his arms.

"The computer in Washington will tell us when we've hit the right code," Waverly said.

The screen went blank for a moment, then began to fill. Ralph, who still couldn't read the jade-green letters, was transfixed by the little square dot that towed the lines across the screen, left to right, left to right, row after row. Whenever it finished pulling out a line it had to run back and pull out the next. He felt a kinship with that little square dot.

When the screen was full, it went blank again and started over, presumably with fresh code words. It filled sixteen times in the first half hour by Ralph's count. He had no idea how many times it filled within the next, because by the end of it his attention had wandered. Modern detective work, he decided, was as interesting as scratching one's own balls, with none of the satisfaction.

Twenty minutes into the second hour, the little dot stopped as if to rest, flashing on and off.

"Crapped out," said Neal. "Any other suggestions?"

"Try 'Federal government,' " Waverly suggested.

"Uh-uh. We'd be here for a month."

" 'Carpenter,' " said Ralph.

The screen tripped out information for thirty seconds.

Neal said, "Ten Carpenters with the D.C. regional office. Six file clerks, two of them women, two couriers, a field operative, and an assistant regional director."

"Try the field operative."

"Carpenter, Howard P." Neal tapped out the name, waited. " 'Deceased 3/10/87.' "

"Shit. Try the assistant director."

He did. " 'Carpenter, James A. Born Camden, N.J., 9/22/38, father—' "

"Too old. The couriers."

One was in his early twenties. The other was black.

"I thought they couldn't put nothing about race in a personnel file."

"The applicant doesn't have to," Waverly said. "The interviewer can, for statistical purposes."

"What's left?" Ralph asked.

"Four male file clerks, from the first names," said Neal.

"Run 'em."

Of the four, two were black. The third, Christian name Morgan, was on maternity leave for six months. Alvin Carpenter, the one remaining, matched the Carpenter Ralph knew in race, sex, age, and height, but not in weight.

"He looked like he's been sick. Ask it where he is now."

The screen changed. "It says he's on temporary reassignment to Anchorage."

"A blind. Feed in Bishop Philip Steelcase, see do we get a match."

"Interface," Waverly corrected.

"In yours, you little pisspot. What'd I do to you?"

"Computer terminology, Mr. Poteet."

"Oh."

Neal said, "The machine says it doesn't know Steelcase from Fred's donkey."

"Cover-up," said Ralph.

"Who would use a file clerk to commit murder?"

"Who'd send one to Alaska? What's he going to file, polar bears? He's no more a file clerk than I am."

"Mr. Poteet, you *are* a file clerk."

"Not since Lucy Loveapples fired me."

Neal said, "I thought you quit."

Ralph pointed at the screen. "How do we get this thing to spill its guts?"

"Enter 'Dismas,' " Waverly said.

Neal looked at him. "What's that?"

"It isn't a what, it's a who. Dismas was the thief who died on the cross with Christ. He's the patron saint of thieves and clandestine activities."

Neal went on looking at him.

"I mean, since we're talking about the Church."

"Give it a whirl," Ralph said.

Waverly spelled the name and Neal entered it. The screen changed again.

"Well, well," Neal said.

"Wow," Waverly said.

"What?" Ralph demanded.

Neal sat back. "Don't tell me you can't read *that*."

Ralph leaned forward and squinted. Neal was right. Glowing greenly and plainly in the center of the screen was the single word: ABSOLUTION.

Chapter 21

"*H*ow'd you know to try 'Dismas'?" Neal asked Waverly.

"Just a hunch. The Church was involved, so it was a possibility. There may be more than one security code, depending upon how many people are in on it; if so, that reduced the odds against us finding our way in."

Ralph asked, "How'd you even hear about Dismas?"

"I had a religious aunt."

"Yeah? I don't see no marks."

"Marks? Oh. Heavens, no. Aunt Cora wouldn't swat a mosquito."

"She wasn't so religious, then. So what's 'Absolution' mean?"

"In the Catholic faith—"

Ralph grasped Waverly by his necktie. "I been up to my ass in Catholics since Monday. If I hear one more lousy mea culpa from you I'll perform extreme unction on your face. What I want to know is what's 'Absolution' got to do with two dead priests, one dead landlord, and a Kentucky fried hooker."

"Okay," said Waverly in an E.T. voice. He was choking.

Neal said, "You know, this doesn't do much for your claim that you didn't strangle Vinnie."

Ralph let go. "Sorry, kid. Ain't nobody had a day like mine since Job."

"No harm done, Mr. Poteet." He stood sucking in air.

"Feed 'Absolution' into that thing and see what it shits out," Ralph told Neal.

"You got a way with words, Ralph." He tapped out the code. "Uh-oh."

"What?" Ralph couldn't read the response.

" 'This file Priority One Confidential. Enter secondary access code.' "

"More passwords?"

"I'm going to try 'Catholic Church.' "

"Stop!" Waverly grasped Neal's wrist before he could begin striking keys. "Ask it if the file has a safeguard."

"What's a safeguard?" Ralph asked.

Neal said, "It's like an alarm in case someone tries to break into a file." He entered the question. "Uh-oh."

"Safeguard?"

"Yeah."

"Can't you get around it?"

"I won't try."

"Why the hell not?"

"Because I got no way of knowing what kind of safeguard it is. Some of them not only shut you out, they also record your attempt to break in and run an automatic trace. In an hour we could be up to our eyebrows in cops."

"Shit," Ralph said. "It's getting so a grifter can't make a dollar. We might as well be living in Russia."

"Well, we learned something," Neal said.

"Like what?"

"You're in even deeper shit than I figured. What do you plan to do?"

"Find out what's Absolution, what else?"

Neal laughed. "I can see the headline now: 'P.I. Found Slain; Sought Absolution.' "

"Funny guy." He looked at Waverly. "So, kid, you learn anything about the detective business?"

"It can be frustrating, can't it?"

"It's a bitch. Can you say 'bitch,' kid?"

Waverly lifted his chin. "Mrs. Lovechild discourages profanity. She says it's a sign of a minimal education and low intelligence."

"Kid, I never knew how to cuss till I met Gus Lovechild. How you going to get in with folks if you don't speak the language?"

"Mrs. Lovechild says a Lovechild operative should stand above the crowd, not bring himself down to its level."

"Next time she says something like that, tell her to go fuck herself."

He colored. "She'd fire me."

Ralph looked at Neal. "What's that on his face?"

"He's blushing. You wouldn't recognize it."

"Come on, kid. Didn't you ever once want to say or do something that'd make Goosey Lucy's panties ride up?"

"Well."

"Spit it out. It's good for the gut."

"Only when she comes to work with that ruffled thing around her neck. It makes her look like a Victorian turtle."

Ralph laughed. "Tell her."

"I couldn't."

"You got to. Otherwise that stuff keeps building up till it comes out your ass and you'll be carrying around one of them inflatable inner tubes for the rest of your life."

"You better listen to him," Neal said. "Ralph knows his assholes."

"Thanks, Mr. Poteet. I'll remember."

Neal shut down the system and stood. "Where do you go from here, Ralph?"

oooooo

"I got a place to hole up. Can I get a lift to Ann Arbor?"

"You won't know till you stand out front and stick your thumb out."

"Come on, Neal."

"What happened to your car?"

"I gave it to a bum."

"I bet it never knew the difference."

"The police recovered it," Waverly said. "I heard it on the radio. They found it abandoned."

"How about you, kid? I bet you're busting to take somebody for a spin in that Rabbit."

Waverly puckered his forehead. "Isn't that—?"

"Aiding and abetting and accessory after the fact of murder," Neal finished. "Knowing Ralph is a treasure trove of once-in-a-lifetime experiences."

"You should turn yourself in, Mr. Poteet. The sooner you do that, the sooner you'll clear your name."

"Right now it ain't my name I want to get clear."

"Leave the kid alone. You already made a burglar out of him."

Waverly reached for the telephone by the keyboard. "I'll call a cab."

"Tell them to pick me up on the corner."

Ten minutes later, Ralph stood on the corner, hands in his pockets and shoulders hunched against the cold. Neal had left first and Waverly had stayed behind to rearm the burglar alarm. Ralph had Absolution on his mind, surely a first.

A pair of bright headlights swung around the corner and slowed, blinding him momentarily. He stepped forward and grasped the cab's door handle. At that instant he realized it wasn't attached to a cab at all, but to a black station wagon, whose driver stuck his martyr's emaciated face and head of stubbly hair out the window and said, "Get in." Carpenter's hand was wrapped around the butt of a silenced automatic resting on the windowsill.

Chapter 22

*T*o his knowledge, Ralph had been in the presence of a genuine killer only once, when while representing Great Lakes Universal Life, Casualty, Auto, and Paternity, he happened to be in the living room of a widow whose husband had died of a respiratory disorder when the police came and arrested her for feeding him cyanide. Ralph had read somewhere that you could see it in their eyes, but he had been staring at her breasts, and since at the time he was preoccupied with the fact that he had just drunk a highball prepared by her, he had taken note of little else after the arrest. He had not had a mixed drink since, as they were all caught up in his mind with stomach pumps and the emergency room at Detroit Receiving. More to the point, he had concluded that writers who claimed that about eyes were probably full of shit.

It was in Carpenter's eyes, though; yawning behind the large black irises like open graves.

Ralph had no idea how long he stood there, staring at the man with the closely shorn head and general appearance of figures Ralph had seen in paintings of the Crucifixion, at the wheel of a vehicle that bore too close a resemblance to a hearse to be mere coincidence. Long enough, he reasoned, to ruffle even Carpenter's patience, for he made one of those gestures that can only be made with a gun and told Ralph again to get into the car.

"Good night, Mr. Poteet."

Whether it was the sudden imposition of Chuck Waverly's youthful voice or the brilliance of the Volkswagen's headlights as the car swung out of the alley next to Lovechild Confidential Inquiries, Carpenter blinked and took his attention off Ralph. In that instant, Ralph threw his bulk into action: scuttling down the sidewalk, clawing open the Rabbit's door on the passenger's side, piling into the seat next to the startled young operative.

"Gun it, kid."

"Huh?"

Grunting, Ralph swung a leg over the shift console and squashed his foot down on top of Waverly's on the accelerator. The little engine mounted behind the backseat wailed. The car didn't budge.

"Take your foot off the fucking clutch."

"Yessir."

The car lurched ahead and stalled.

"Put it in low," Ralph said calmly.

Waverly depressed the clutch and downshifted, banging the lever into Ralph's testicles. Through a haze of pain Ralph watched Carpenter barreling out the driver's door of the black station wagon, automatic in hand.

"Start the car," Ralph said.

The engine ground into life.

"Go."

This time Waverly released the clutch smoothly as he pressed down the accelerator. As he pulled around the station wagon, Carpenter stood in front of the Rabbit, bracing the gun in both hands police-style. Waverly started to slow down, but Ralph tramped on his foot again. Tires chirped, Carpenter filled the windshield. At the last instant he threw himself out of the Volkswagen's path. Ralph leaned on Waverly's foot. In the sport mirror on the right side of the car he saw Carpenter, growing smaller by the second, scramble to his feet and make for the open door of the station wagon.

"What'll this crate do?"

"Speedometer says eighty."

"Fuck the speedometer."

"Where are we going?"

"Anywhere that creep behind us ain't."

After two blocks Ralph returned his leg to his side of the console and nursed his groin. Waverly drove with his hands at ten and two on the steering wheel and signaled all his turns. As he prepared to stop for a red light, Ralph reached over and rapped him on the side of his head. The young man understood the gesture and sped through the intersection. Fortunately, there was no crossing traffic.

Although it was still early evening, not many cars were out. When a pair of headlights appeared several blocks behind them, Ralph knew they were Carpenter's.

"Take St. Antoine to Woodward and get on I-94 westbound," Ralph said. "And lay off the goddamn turn signal."

"Yessir. Sir?"

"Yeah?"

"Is that the man you were telling us about?"

"No, he's my ex-wife. She went and got a sex change operation and now she's after me for back alimony. Oh, shit."

Police strobe lights were flashing on the entrance ramp to the interstate, where a semi lay on its side across the mouth like the last dinosaur.

"Cut over and take the southbound Lodge," Ralph said. "Kind of hurry." The station wagon's headlights had gained a block on them.

"Southbound Lodge is closed for construction."

"Son of a bitch, I forgot. Turn here."

They tore down a side street.

"Keep turning. That gas hog's got us for speed, but this bucket can outmaneuver it into next Tuesday."

Waverly was a competent driver, taking sharp corners without slowing down or damaging pedestrians. Ralph saw neighborhoods he hadn't visited in years. The town was funny that way: a million and a half people, and every one of them wore his own little rut and never departed from it. Carpenter's lights had long since disappeared from the mirror.

"I think we've lost him," Waverly said.

"Probably cut his lights." But as they continued on their corkscrew course, Ralph believed they had left their pursuer far behind. He popped open the glove compartment. "You got a bottle in here?"

"I don't drink."

"Kids today." Closing the compartment, he took a pull from his flask, which he had transferred to his hip pocket before giving his suitcoat to Homeless. He took another pull, then put away the flask and adjusted his seat, subsiding against the cushions. After a moment he chuckled.

"What's funny, Mr. Poteet?"

"Just that hooker back there on the corner."

"The one in the cowboy hat and go-go boots?"

"Texas Annie. She's been there longer than the streetlight. They tried busting her once, but she called the Detroit Historical Society and got herself declared a historic spot."

"Really?"

Ralph chuckled again. "Drive, Kato. Take Jefferson to Cadieux and climb on the westbound I-94 from there." He tilted his hat over his eyes.

"Mr. Poteet?"

He came awake slowly. He'd been dreaming that the governor had appointed him state treasurer. "Just fill the bag," he muttered. "No small bills."

"Mr. Poteet?"

He realized they'd stopped. Sitting up, he tipped back his hat and looked at the black station wagon parked across the I-94 entrance ramp. "Holy shit."

"He must have seen us slow down at the other one," Waverly said. "What should we do?"

"Burn ass!"

Waverly hurled the Rabbit into a U-turn, tires shrilling as he came out of it and fishtailed back the way they had come. In the mirror, the station wagon's lights raked the sides of the street, turning.

Cadieux dead-ended at Lake Shore Drive, an extension of Jefferson. "Which way?" Waverly asked.

"Pick one. Jesus Christ."

They turned left. To their right, the India-ink surface of Lake St. Clair at night rippled under a broken yellow moon, while to their left the residential neighborhoods of affluent Grosse Pointe grew less dense, the houses becoming larger and spaced farther apart, surrounded by great sweeping lawns that looked black under decorative gas lamps. Behind them, a dark car with its headlights off gleamed in the moonlight reflecting from the water.

"Turn in there," Ralph directed.

The route indicated was a curving composition driveway between stone gateposts, leading to a white Georgian mansion with all its windows lit. Waverly hesitated before turning.

"Step on it. Looks like a party. Even Carpenter wouldn't try anything in a bunch of swells."

A uniformed parking attendant Waverly's age stepped down eagerly from the long porch, paused when the little Volkswagen slid fully into view behind a line of Bentleys, Jaguars, and Eldorados, and leaned a disappointed face down to the window on Ralph's side.

"You with the serving staff?" the attendant asked.

Ralph looked back down the driveway, at the end of which the black station wagon had stopped. "Yeah," he said.

"Take it around back."

Behind the house they parked beside a white van with MAR-TY'S PARTIES painted in elegant script along its sides. A black maid with white-rimmed glasses let them in the back door. "Kitchen's that way."

The kitchen was as big as a ballroom, paved with stainless steel and men and women in white aprons and serving uniforms. The air smelled of radicchio and anchovies and other small weird foods preferred by the wealthy. A tall man, balding in front, wearing a black cutaway and white shirtboard, studied Ralph and Waverly from head to foot with predatory eyes.

"Was there an accident?" he asked.

Ralph said, "We always look like this. What do you want us to do, Mac?"

"To begin with, I don't want you to call me Mac." The tall man flung open a cupboard and removed two short gold jackets from hangers inside. "Put these on. Then pick up two of those trays of canapés and serve them in the parlor. Go through the swinging door and turn right. You do know which way right is."

"I go by my dick. What do you use?"

The tall man sighed. "My father begged me to go into the vinegar business with him. I said I wanted to work with people."

Ralph's jacket was too long in the sleeves and wouldn't fasten around his middle. He gave up and hoisted one of the silver trays aligned on a stainless steel sideboard. "So what's the shindig?"

"The annual convention of the F.A.N.A.P.B.B. and T. Don't they tell you fellows anything?"

"Sounds like a wet fart. What's it stand for?" Ralph headed for the swinging door.

"The Fraternal Association of North American Pit Bull Breeders and Trainers."

Chuck Waverly caught Ralph's tray. The young man's jacket hung on his slender frame like bunting and now a canapé clung to one lapel like a barnacle.

"Clumsy idiot!" said the tall man. "Are you filling in for someone competent?"

Ralph said, "Sorry. What do these guys do, like get together and talk about their dogs?"

"Of course not. It's a dog show."

"Let me get this straight. You're sending us into a room full of pit bulls, carrying food."

"There hasn't been an incident in two years."

"What happened two years ago?"

The tall man made a gesture of exaggerated impatience. " 'We have nothing to fear but fear itself.' Franklin Delano Roosevelt."

Ralph thrust his tray into the tall man's hands. " 'Fuck you, Tony.' Lyndon LaRouche."

"What about Carpenter?" Waverly asked.

"Let *him* carry in the can of peas."

"Canapés," corrected the tall man. "Are you going to do your job or not? If the answer is no, you're in the way and I'll have to ask you to leave."

"Do we get to keep the jackets?"

"Out! Get out!"

"Okay, okay. Gimme the munchies. You sissies got no sense of humor."

The tall man gave him the tray. "There's really nothing to be concerned about. Pit bulls are very well behaved, so long as they don't smell fear."

Ralph said, "Which way's downwind?"

Chapter 23

*T*wenty minutes later, Ralph and Waverly, their pantslegs shredded and their gold jackets in tatters, spilled into the kitchen and shoved the door shut against the snarling and scrabbling of claws on the other side. Ralph was missing his right shoe.

"What happened?" demanded the tall balding man in the black cutaway.

Leaving Waverly to hold the door shut, Ralph placed a shoulder against the big butcher block in the center of the room and started pushing. "Help me get this thing in front of the door."

The tall man gestured and two liveried servants put their hands and shoulders to the task. When the door was blocked, Waverly and Ralph collapsed against it. The noise on the other side was fearsome.

"It was the fucking rum balls," Ralph explained. "They do the same thing every time."

"You were supposed to serve them, not eat them," said the tall man. "Do what?"

Waverly said, "He makes cat noises."

"Cat noises?"

"You know, meowing and spitting. It was the best imitation those dogs ever heard."

"Pit bulls got no sense of humor," Ralph said.

The tall man glared at the serving staff. "Who is responsible for these idiots?"

Nobody spoke.

"This is a disaster. Nothing like this has ever happened at the annual convention of the F.A.N.A.P.B.B. and T."

"What about two years ago?" Ralph asked.

"That was nothing. Mrs. Chubwallader was chased into the pool by Prince Albert. A really first-rate animal, but he couldn't stand the smell of Giorgio."

"That'd be *Mr.* Crumwallader?"

"*Chub*wallader. Giorgio is a perfume. Mrs. Chubwallader has been widowed for forty-seven years. She owns this house. You should know that. Where are your copies of the work order?"

"I think Prince Albert ate them."

"Indeed. Collier's Domestics will hear of this."

"What's that, a kennel?"

"Collier's Domestics is your employer. Or perhaps not. Who are you?"

Ralph drew himself up, trying not to stand lopsided on his shoeless foot. "I'm Bruce Wayne and this here's Dick Grayson. We're with Animal Control. We got a tip you folks was exceeding your pit bull capacity and we came here undercover to find out was it true. Ain't that right, kid?" He nudged Waverly, who jerked upright.

"Down! I mean, yes sir."

"*What* pit bull capacity?" The tall man's brow was puckered.

"Grosse Pointe City Ordinance number ex-ex-eye-eye-eye, subparagraph B: 'No residential establishment shall be in excess of one pit bull per square yard.' On account of they get pissed in crowds. You can look it up yourself."

○○○○○○

"And what did you find out?"

"You squeaked by this time. Well, we got to go file our report. Let's go, kid."

The tall man gestured again. One of the kitchen staff, a large black man in an apron and chef's cap holding a cleaver, stepped in front of the back door. "Where are your credentials?" asked the tall man.

"Man wants credentials."

Waverly made a sickly grin. He appeared on the verge of hysteria.

"What's funny?" asked the tall man.

"Us guys on pit bull detail leave our badges in the office when we go undercover. You don't want to startle no dogs by flashing something shiny."

"I suppose that makes sense."

"It does? I mean, sure it does." Ralph pointed a stern finger. "Remember what I said. One dog per square yard, no more."

"Just one moment."

Ralph paused in front of the man with the cleaver. He and Waverly were leaning on each other.

The tall man wrung his hands, something Ralph had never actually seen anyone do before. "What about those?"

As he said *those*, something heavy hurled itself against the swinging door on the other side, buckling the edges. A copper pot fell clattering off the wall.

"Throw 'em a maid." Ralph jammed his heel down on the black man's instep. As he stooped, gasping, Ralph shoved him off balance, seized Waverly's arm, and hustled outside.

There was no sign of the station wagon. Ralph put Waverly into the passenger's seat, for the young man was in no condition to drive, and slid behind the wheel. The accelerator felt cold under his stockinged foot. As he turned the key, something just as cold touched the base of his skull.

From behind the seat, Carpenter said, "Drive."

○○○○○○

Waverly laughed.

"Shut up, kid," Ralph said. The laughter stopped. "How'd a beanpole like you scrunch himself into that teensy backseat?" Ralph asked.

"Just drive."

"I ain't too good with these foreign jobs."

The gun nudged him. "Learn."

Ralph started the engine. "Where to?"

"Straight to hell if you don't put this thing in gear right now."

Ralph pressed down the accelerator and released the clutch. The little car shot forward, bumped up three steps, found traction on the back porch, and tore loose the kitchen doorframe heading inside. The tall man, the man with the cleaver, and the rest of the kitchen and serving staff scattered. The Volkswagen struck the butcher block hard and stalled. Carpenter piled into the back of Ralph's seat and fell to the floor of the car.

Waverly was sprawled in the passenger's seat, having stunned himself when the top of his head hit the windshield. Ralph left him where he was, tumbling out of the car and pulling himself grunting on top of the butcher block in front of the swinging door. Carpenter started out behind him, gun in hand.

There was a brief pause after Ralph pushed open the swinging door. Then the first of the pit bulls lunged through the opening, clawed for a purchase, and bounded over the top of the butcher block. Another flew over its back, and within thirty seconds half a dozen dogs had gained snarling, foaming access to the kitchen, with five more fighting for their turn. Big, square-muscled brutes with pointed ears and muzzles shaped like howitzers, they ranged in color from white to rusty brown and in temperament from casual bloodlust to uncontrolled rage. They reminded Ralph a little of his father.

As for Ralph, after shoving open the door he had curled both hands over its top and ridden it into the short corridor outside the kitchen. He shared it with a number of upset dog owners and a very old pit bull that had been introduced to him earlier as Emperor Maximilian. Too fat and ancient to take part in the frenzy, Maximilian lay in the middle of the floor with his white-whiskered chin resting on his paws, chewing unconcernedly on the leg of a Louis XIV occasional table.

"Nixon! Richard Milhouse Nixon!" called a buxom woman with blue rinse in her hair and wattles. "Whatever can that dog be after?"

"Probably a new name," said Ralph.

Amid the confusion behind him, he heard a loud report, but whether it belonged to Carpenter's automatic or a car door as he shut himself off from the dogs, Ralph couldn't tell. He had a fleeting sense of guilt for having left Chuck Waverly behind; but this was how youngsters learned, and in any case nobody's skin was dearer to Ralph than Ralph's. On his way through the parlor, he helped himself to a handful of rum balls and washed them down with brandy from an abandoned snifter. Fuel.

Chapter 24

*A*pril Dane answered the door of her apartment wearing two towels. Unfortunately for Ralph's unpredictable libido, the one she had wrapped around her body was no larger than the one she wore turban-fashion on her head. Ralph's body reacted instantly. April looked down and smiled. "Glad to see me?"

He managed a crooked grin, which was the only kind he ever had. "How do you think I pushed the buzzer?"

"What happened to your left shoe?" Her gaze had flicked below his torn pants; he'd ditched the jacket before hailing a cab.

"I just came from a pit bull convention."

"Okay, don't tell me."

"No, really."

"What were you doing at a pit bull convention?"

"Pissing my pants and running like hell. Can I come in?"

"With a line like that, who could resist?" She stepped aside and closed the door behind him. She smelled of fresh soap and warm skin.

"You getting ready to go out?"

"No, just taking a shower before bed."

ooooooo

"You're kidding."

"Don't you ever wash up before turning in?"

"Why waste soap if nobody's going to smell you?"

She stepped forward and wrapped her arms around his neck. Beads of moisture glittered on her bare shoulders. "You're smelling me."

"I ain't in the mood."

"Your lips say no, no, no, but . . ." She bumped him.

"Your *on* button's stuck, that it?"

"Let's see what happens when we push yours."

"Jesus."

Sometime later, Ralph lay hyperventilating in April's bed. April snored prettily with her head on his chest and one bare thigh slung across his groin. He wanted to check his pulse, but was afraid of waking her. He decided that Lyla the professional could not be like her sister the amateur, or she wouldn't be living in a crummy building like Ralph's.

Lying there in the dark, waiting for his blood to stop racing, he wondered how Chuck Waverly had fared with the dogs and Carpenter. It worried him more that he should wonder at all. The old Ralph wouldn't; but even he couldn't stand up to his pecker in dead landlords and clergymen for an extended period and not come away changed.

The telephone rang. He jumped.

April, still asleep, made a feline noise of protest and nestled her head deeper into the graying hairs on Ralph's chest. He knew it was the police calling; trouble had its own ring. They had traced him there from Grosse Pointe. He wondered if there was a penalty for impersonating an Animal Control officer, and if it would matter once they finished sentencing him for Vinnie's murder and the destruction of a Grosse Pointe kitchen.

"Phone's ringing," he said.

April slept on.

OOOOOO

His determination to ignore the bell eroded in direct relation to the number of times it rang. He wished he had a matchstick. Finally he freed himself from the naked girl's embrace and stumbled, just as naked, over to the low dresser where the telephone stood.

"Poteet?"

He felt his private parts shriveling. He had recognized the sepulchral voice instantly. He slammed down the receiver. After a pause the ringing began again.

"Get that, will you?" muttered April.

Ralph stood in a puddle of sweat on the floor. The noise was like the clanging of bells at his own funeral. He had to stop it.

"Don't hang up again," Carpenter said.

"How'd you track me down?"

"That isn't important."

"What'd you do, ice the kid?"

"If you mean your young friend, he's at Detroit General, getting a distemper shot. He was bitten on the ankle."

"What'd he taste like?"

"Never mind that. I want to talk to you."

"Who's your interpreter, Smith and Wesson?"

"No guns. I'll meet you wherever you like, as long as it's tonight."

"That what you said to the bishop?"

"The bishop's part of what I want to talk to you about."

"So talk."

"Not over the telephone."

Ralph said, "You can't see me, so I'll tell you what I'm doing. I got the phone in one hand and I'm pointing one finger of the other at the ceiling, and I ain't asking to go to the toilet. That clear enough, or should I send you a picture?"

"Pictures are what I want to talk about."

"I ain't interested. What do I have to do, moon you from the top of the Renaissance Center?"

"I'll pay you a thousand dollars just to meet with me."

Ralph scratched his butt. The gesture stimulated his thinking. "Cash?"

"Big or small bills?"

"Make 'em small. I like a nice fat wallet."

"Will you meet with me?"

"The thousand's just to talk, right? I don't let no pictures go for no crummy grand."

"Just to talk."

"Somebody's going to know where I am. If I don't check in by a certain time, the pictures go to the cops."

"When and where do you want to meet?"

"I know just the place," Ralph said.

After giving Carpenter directions, Ralph hung up and called Neal English.

"Hello. Jesus."

"Not even close," said Ralph.

"It's almost two!"

"Thanks. Before you say go away, I want you to clear the pillow fuzz out of your ears and listen. I just talked to Carpenter."

"You having some work done?"

"Not *a* carpenter, asshole. Carpenter. The file clerk that runs around filing people under DOA, remember?"

There was a pause. "Listen, if you're laying someplace bleeding, call nine-one-one. I got to go to work in the morning."

"The conversation was over the phone. I'm meeting him in an hour to talk about the pictures."

"What pictures?"

"The Loch Ness monster's dick, shit-for-brains. What pictures you think?"

"Oh, yeah, the monsignor. I almost forgot about those. What's he paying?"

"I don't know yet. He just wants to talk about them."

"What's he paying to talk?"

"What makes it he's paying?"

"He kills people and you got a yellow streak as wide as the Rouge. But you'd sell your right thumb for a buck and change. How much?"

"Five hundred."

"Bullshit."

"Okay, seven-fifty."

"I get half."

"Sure, Neal. I'd never screw a partner."

"*Ex*-partner. And I been screwed by you so many times I whistle when I fart. When you going to check in?"

"Say five o'clock."

"Say seven. I told you, I got to go to work in the morning."

"I could be dead."

"You won't be any deader at seven o'clock than at five. Where's the meet?"

"Richard's. You know Richard."

"He still got that fucking dog?"

"Yeah."

"Better take along a can of Glade." Neal hung up.

As Ralph replaced the receiver, April giggled. She was wide awake now. "Is that the way you always dress when you use the phone?"

He looked down at himself. "That reminds me. You got any shoes my size?"

Chapter 25

*R*alph took off his hat to fan away the stench. "Richard, I thought you was going to stop feeding that mutt cabbage."

"I tried. He won't eat nothing else." As the one-armed black bartender spoke, Coleman the Doberman stretched himself on his rug behind the bar and passed gas in both directions. Richard squashed out a cigarette butt smoldering in an ashtray on the bar. "Can't be too careful. Say, I heard you was wanted."

"You going to turn me in?"

"Far as I'm concerned, this bar is Switzerland. Usual?"

"Make it gin, straight up. Over there." Ralph pointed to the booth farthest from Coleman—he had had enough of dogs for one night, flatulent or otherwise—and headed that way, shuffling in April's fuzzy pink slippers, which were too small for him.

"Nice shoes."

"Fuck you."

But for Ralph, the bar contained only three customers: Andy the retard, guzzling Pepto-Bismol in his customary booth and marking up his antebellum copy of *TV Guide*, and two girls in their late teens with orange and magenta hair, sharing a table by the door and blue stories over green drinks with yellow flowers floating on top.

"Place is quiet," said Ralph, when Richard brought Ralph's gin to his table. "Ain't the graveyard shift at the *News* getting out about now?"

"The scribes don't much come in here no more. Say the place is too smoky."

"You're shitting me."

Richard shrugged.

"How about the four-to-midnight down at the steering gear plant?"

"Strictly club soda and spinach pie in the Capistrano Lounge."

"Jesus."

"Face it, Ralph. In a Waterford world, you're a Dixie cup."

Ralph drank off half his gin. One of the teenage girls left money for their drinks from a roll the size of a shot put and the two went out. "You still got that sawed-off behind the bar?" Ralph asked Richard.

"It ain't worth shooting yourself over."

"It ain't me I want to shoot."

"That don't matter neither. I still got to mop up the blood." He snapped the bar rag at a cockroach on the table. "You in trouble besides what I know about?"

Ralph laughed, took off his hat, ran his fingers through his thinning hair, and put the hat back on. "A few days ago, the world wasn't so stinking. I went to work, got yelled at by the boss, spent the day doing a job a chimp could do if the pay was decent, got drunk, went home to an apartment the size of a belly button, passed out. One morning I answered the phone. Since then I been doped, chased, busted, fucked, stuck guns at, almost burned, and throwed to the dogs. I'm out of a job. I'm wanted for murder, so I can't go home. I got an appointment with a killer. I don't even own a pair of shoes. My life's always been shit, but lately there's blood in it. What makes you think I'm in trouble?"

"You're complaining 'cause you got fucked?"

He sighed. "Richard, you're a piss-poor bartender. You never listen. You got any idea why I keep coming here?"

" 'Cause you been throwed out of every other bar in the greater metropolitan area. You want another hit?"

"What I want is the sawed-off. If you won't give it to me, I wish you'd stand next to it and keep an eye on this joker I'm meeting. You can't miss him. He looks like Vincent Price with AIDS."

Richard scratched his stump. "You ain't dealing no drugs in my bar."

"How long you know me?"

"You want me to check your tab?"

"No drugs. No white slavery."

The bartender grinned. "Hell, *white*'s okay. Just don't bleed on my floor." He returned to the bar.

Ralph nursed the rest of his gin. He wanted to finish it and order another, but wanted a clear head more. He wished his revolver weren't in police lockup. More than that he wished that the next time a hooker found a priest dead in her bed she'd call anybody but him. He watched the cockroach Richard had exiled drag its bashed body back across the table and pull itself laboriously up the side of Ralph's glass. Its wings were broken and two of its legs weren't working. Ralph let it get to the rim, then snapped it away with a forefinger and swatted it with his hat when it landed on top of the seat opposite, flattening it. He wasn't quite so far gone he had started to feel any kinship with bugs.

"Poteet."

He knocked over the glass, but caught it before any of its contents could spill out. He hadn't noticed when Carpenter came in from the street and lowered himself into the other seat. He looked gaunter than ever in the same black overcoat buttoned to the neck; not unlike the roach lying in squashed state just behind his head. His ears stuck out slightly and his skin had a yellowish cast. Ralph noticed that his hands were torn and bleeding.

"You ain't chewed up so bad." Ralph, seeking nonchalance, picked up his drink and swirled it. A drop flew into his good eye and burned there.

"Pit bulls are overrated. A grown man in good condition can overpower almost any number of them if he keeps his head. Your friend did not, but he'll be okay. I stayed with him until the ambulance came."

Ralph rubbed his eye. "I didn't know you mechanics cared."

"Mechanic?"

"Let's cut the crap. How'd you find me?"

"I called all the cab companies and offered a reward to the driver who remembered picking up a fare near Lake Shore Drive at about the time you left the mansion. You shouldn't have had him drop you off right in front of the place you were staying."

"I didn't feel like doing a whole hell of a lot of walking in just one shoe. What'd you do, call every apartment in the building?"

"Fortunately, you answered on my third try."

Carpenter's deep tones chilled Ralph; they were like clods of earth striking the lid of a coffin. He drank some gin. "Where's the grand?"

The gaunt man drew a long envelope from inside his coat, lifted the flap, and showed Ralph the thick sheaf of bills inside. When Ralph reached for it he pulled it back. Ralph subsided into his seat.

"You want to talk, talk," he said. "Can I get you a drink? I bet it's cold in Alaska this time of year."

"I imagine it is. But why should I care?"

"Have it your way, Alvin. Okay if I call you Alvin?"

"Who's Alvin?"

Everything about the man made Ralph's balls wither. He fortified himself with another sip, put on his crooked grin. "I said no more crap. I know all about you, Alvin. You're a file clerk for the Justice Department, and you're supposed to be in Anchorage. But then a shooter's gotta be somewhere, and he can't put down 'hit man' on his income tax form."

"Peter is my Christian name. I've never known anyone named Alvin. And I don't work for the Justice Department."

"CIA, then. What's it matter to a hitter who pays his bills or what name's on the check?"

"I don't work for the CIA. I'm not connected with the federal government at all."

"Freelance?"

Carpenter reached inside his coat again. "Richard!" shouted Ralph, and ducked under the table.

Life was peaceful there. He saw that the linoleum was torn and that forty-seven people who chewed gum had used the underside of the table for a parking space.

"Poteet?"

Carpenter's features upside down were no less unnerving. Ralph had no place to go from there. Cautiously, he crawled out into the open. Andy, in his booth, was finishing his Pepto-Bismol over an article about Mary Tyler Moore. Richard was reading the *Free Press* classifieds behind the bar. There wasn't a weapon in sight. Ralph took his seat.

"What was that about?" Carpenter asked.

"I thought you was going for that piece of yours."

"You mean this?" Carpenter took the automatic out of his pocket.

This time, Ralph stayed under the table until the gaunt man joined him. Squatting, he handed him the gun. Ralph turned it over. It was blue plastic, a water pistol.

"What was you going to do, shove it up my nose and try to drown me?"

"I don't like guns. As a matter of fact, they frighten me. I only used it before because you're a hard man to pin down."

"You're scared of guns?"

○○○○○○

"Terrified."

"You ought to look for another line of work."

"I'm not a hit man."

"What the hell *are* you?"

"If you'll sit still a minute I'll show you." Again he reached inside his coat. This time he withdrew a brown leather folder and opened it under Ralph's nose. It contained an impressive-looking card identifying Peter Paul Carpenter as a correspondent for the *Washington Post*.

Chapter 26

"**W**here's Alvin?" Ralph asked after a moment.

"In Alaska, I suppose." Carpenter put away the folder. "Who gave you that information?"

"A fucking computer."

Richard came over and squatted on his haunches to look at the pair of men under the table. "What can I get you gents? Gin? Scotch? Mop 'n' Glo?"

Ralph and Carpenter crawled out and took their seats. "Hit me again," Ralph said. To Carpenter: "You?"

"I don't drink."

"You ain't no reporter!"

"Hold it down." Carpenter ordered a Coke. When Richard left: "Are we talking or not? If not, I can use the thousand."

"Who shot the bishop?" Ralph asked.

"I was going to ask you the same thing."

"Who strangled Vinnie?"

"I was going to ask you the same thing."

"Who burned Lyla Dane?"

"I was going—"

Ralph raised the water pistol. "What *do* you know?"

"I was going to ask you the same thing."

Their drinks came. Ralph waited until Richard was back behind the bar. "I got to know some things first. I figure I earned it."

"Shoot."

"Don't tempt me." He put down the water pistol. "I called a phone number I found in the rectory at St. Balthazar. Willard Newton answered. Know who he is?"

"The U.S. attorney general."

"You're the first one who got that right."

"I should hope so. He's the man the *Post* is investigating."

"Investigating for what?"

"I'll need to hear a lot more from you before I give that up."

"When he found out I was calling from Detroit he said, 'Carpenter, I told you never to call me here.' Which Carpenter's that, Alvin or Paul?"

"Peter."

"Who's Peter?"

"*I'm* Peter."

"I thought you was Paul."

"Paul's my middle name."

"I never had one."

"Isaac," Carpenter said.

"What?"

"Ralph Isaac Poteet. I looked you up. Why are you ashamed of it?"

"It ain't the name, it's the initials." Ralph drank. "You was working for Willard Newton, not Bishop Steelcase."

"I'm working for the *Washington Post*. I'm *investigating* Willard Newton."

"Investigating for what?"

"What's Lyla Dane to you?" Carpenter asked.

"Neighbor. She called me to get Monsignor Breame out of her bed."

"But not before you took pictures."

"That was my idea. Hookers got no imagination. You picked up the body for Bishop Steelcase, only you ain't working for him."

"Right. I'm a reporter."

"What kind?"

"Investigative."

"Investigating for what?"

"We did that twice." Carpenter tapped the edge of his glass with the envelope full of bills. "Where are the pictures?"

"You didn't buy no pictures. That money's to talk."

He flipped the envelope into the center of the table. When Ralph reached for it, Carpenter set his glass on top of it. Ralph sat back again.

"Let's see what we got," he said. "You ain't working for Willard Newton, but he thinks you are. You wasn't working for the bishop, but he thought you was. That's why you picked up the body. But you didn't rig Lyla Dane's apartment to blow up in her face."

"Right so far."

"Who drugged me when I was at the bishop's, you or Steelcase?"

"I did. At his orders."

"You went through my pockets and dumped me at Mt. Elliott Cemetery?"

"Yes."

"You went to toss my apartment, found Vinnie already doing that, and squiffed him?"

"No. That was somebody else."

"Who?"

"Maybe I should keep this money," Carpenter said. "I've done more for it than you have. Did you really take pictures, or was that a bluff to blackmail the bishop?"

"I took 'em. I ain't handing 'em over for any lousy grand."

○○○○○○

"Do what you like with them. They're only of peripheral interest."

"Okay, I'll just take my envelope and be on my way." Ralph held out a hand.

"What's your hurry?"

"I like to drink and I don't jog. I figure I got twenty years to live if I don't get shot first and I sure ain't fixing to spend them here smelling Richard's fucking dog."

"So that's what that is. I thought the wind was blowing up from Washington."

"Junior, you sure don't say much for somebody that's paying to talk."

"I'm paying to ask questions, not answer them." Carpenter sipped his Coke and gazed in Andy's direction. "Does he look like a government man to you?"

"The vice president, a little. Around the ass."

"They're always reading."

"What's Absolution?"

Carpenter stared at him. "Where'd you hear about Absolution?"

Ralph felt his grin returning. He sat back and belched juniper.

"Okay. I'm satisfied you've something to trade." The reporter shifted in his seat. "You remember Abscam."

"That thing where all them Democrats got caught with their hands up some camel jockey's burnoose."

"Close enough. In that one, FBI agents posing as Arab nationals induced a number of congressmen to accept bribes for voting their way on trade issues. The transactions were video-taped and used as evidence in court."

"I got to get me one of them cameras," Ralph mused.

"Absolution is the code name for a similar Justice Department operation that went sour."

"What'd they do, run out of sheets?"

"This one was more elaborate, with different targets. The scam involved dressing field agents in clerical robes and placing

○○○○○○

them in confessionals in Catholic parishes believed to include high-ranking figures in organized crime. The plan was to finesse them into incriminating themselves with the use of hidden surveillance equipment."

"You made that up."

"We're pretty sure Willard Newton did. It was his pet scheme."

"It wouldn't hold up in court."

"That's why it was abandoned a year ago. Also it was a disaster from a public relations viewpoint, mixing church and state and all. Not to mention the fact that a large percentage of the newer breed of crime bigwigs is Protestant."

"Royal fuck-up."

"A democratic one, actually. With a small *d*."

"So what's the beef now?"

"There's no such thing as a bureaucratic secret. We had an informant whose conscience got the better of him finally. He contacted our Detroit bureau and they relayed the information to Washington."

"Steelcase?"

"Hardly. We figure he was the one who panicked and called Newton when he got wind of the investigation. I don't think I'll tell you the name of our informant just yet."

Ralph chewed on his swizzle in place of a matchstick. "What'd Newton do?"

"Something he shouldn't have."

"Huh."

"The election's next month. If Willard Newton is linked with a bonehead illegal operation that cost the taxpayers millions, he stands to do more than lose his job. He'll take down the present administration and his entire party with him. So he hired a killer to eliminate the informant."

"You."

"That's what he thinks. Government has nothing on the

Post, Poteet; we've got deep-cover men in some impressive places. Our man in the Justice Department diverted Newton's requisition to us. I got the job of posing as the killer. I'd rather not say why."

"It ain't necessary," Ralph said.

Carpenter was solemn. "Willard Newton violated the First Amendment rights of every confessor who went into one of those booths looking to unburden his soul to someone he thought was a priest. The pilgrims didn't come here for that. Speaking less Constitutionally, I had barely begun my investigation when someone murdered Monsignor Breame."

Ralph had been about to signal Richard for another round. He lowered his hand.

"Breame was our informant," Carpenter said. "You didn't really think he died humping some cheap prostitute, did you?"

Ralph said, "A guy'd have to be pretty low to think a thing like that."

Chapter 27

*R*ichard brought over Ralph's third gin. "Last call, gentlemans. I got to close up and take Coleman out for a crap."

"He won't be able to," Ralph said. "He used up all his gas in here."

Carpenter said, "Nothing for me, thanks."

Richard regarded him. "You feeling okay, mister?"

"I'm fine. Why?"

"Ralph says you got AIDS."

"I didn't neither. You never listen. I said he *looked* like he had it."

"I have an overactive metabolism." Carpenter waited until they were alone again. "Monsignor Breame had a heart condition, hardly unusual in a man with his weight problem. An overdose of digitalis would have brought on a very convincing coronary."

"You saying *Lyla* offed him?" Ralph was incredulous.

"She certainly had opportunity."

"How come the frame? They could of slipped him the mickey in the rectory or anyplace else. Why raise a stink?" Behind the

○○○○○○
185

bar, Coleman chose that unfortunate moment to raise one of his own.

"Our religion editor did some digging. The Vatican was developing an interest in the Detroit archdiocese. Maybe Breame made more than one telephone call. In any case, killing the monsignor and fixing things to look like he died in the saddle would be one way of forestalling a papal investigation. They might even aid in the cover-up."

"There's no way Lyla done it. She called me to get him out of her bed."

"Probably she lost her nerve. That kind of situation brings down a lot of heat on a working girl. So when you called the bishop and told him about Breame, he had no choice but to behave as expected and arrange for the body to be spirited away. It would also explain why an attempt was made on her life the same morning."

"I thought the blast was for me."

"No, whoever wrote the scenario would have known the prostitute they had cast lived alone. What happened to her was her payment for upsetting the applecart."

"Jesus, that's a relief."

"Why? You're the next logical target."

"Yeah, but I got pictures."

Carpenter smiled. The expression transformed his cadaverous features like a bubble in a bottle of formaldehyde. "You're forgetting that they *want* the apparent circumstances of Monsignor Breame's death to come out."

"Oh, yeah." Ralph's pleasant buzz began to recede. "So who's the killer?"

"I was hoping you could tell me."

"Hey, I thought it was you."

"He's good, whoever he is. Assuming we're dealing with only one, which let's hope, his methods range from induced heart attack to arson to strangling to shooting. You don't see too many general practitioners at that level."

○○○○○○

"That's good to know. I wouldn't want to be squiffed by no amateur. Ain't you got files?"

Carpenter nodded. "Impressive ones, too. If he's a corrupt public official as well as a hit man, he's in there."

"You're saying you got nothing?"

"If we had anything, do you think I'd be here?"

Ralph drank. He was beginning to lose his faith in the restorative properties of inexpensive alcohol. "What do we do?"

"What do you mean *we*, paleface?"

"Hey, you need me."

"For what? You obviously know less than I do. But that's the risk I took when I proposed this meeting. Here." He picked up the envelope full of bills and flipped it at Ralph. "If I were you I'd invest in an airline ticket. Say hello to Alvin when you get to Anchorage." He started to rise. Ralph caught his sleeve.

"Okay, you got the pictures."

Carpenter sat back. "Where are they?"

"With a friend."

"That would be Neal English." The formaldehyde formed another bubble. "I said I looked you up."

"What makes you think it ain't some other friend?"

"You have no other friends. Even Neal English is stretching the term. How soon can you get them?"

"As soon as I get back from his place."

"Fine. I'll hold this until then." Carpenter snatched the envelope out of his hand. Ralph made a noise as if his liver had been extracted.

"What do I get when you got the pictures? I already earned the grand by showing up here."

"We can arrange protection."

"What, some cheesy bodyguard?"

"I was thinking more along the lines of using our influence with the local police to hold you as a material witness."

"In *jail*? Fuck that. I can get that by walking out of here and giving myself up."

"And take a shiv between your ribs while you're in the tank. Anyone who would murder a bishop and a monsignor wouldn't be above slipping heroin to some addict to kill an out-of-work detective. Material-witness status will get you a cell to yourself and a guard around the clock."

"Well, I ain't giving up my hole card for county food. If talk's worth a thousand, them pictures gotta be worth five."

"In your dreams. As I said, the pictures are incidental at most."

"Bullshit. Five grand's the price."

Richard appeared at their table with Coleman on a leash. Ralph swore his drink curdled. He gestured understanding and the bartender led the dog to the door to wait.

"I can let you have five hundred," Carpenter said. "I'm over my expense budget as it is."

"Five thousand."

"Six-fifty."

"Okay."

"Okay?"

Ralph shrugged. "Before this week, a hundred was as high as I ever got. A man should know when he's ahead."

"Six-fifty, then. Where should we meet?"

"Give me a number where I can get you and I'll call you from Neal's bank. That's where he put the pictures."

Carpenter gave him the number of the cellular telephone in his station wagon. Ralph borrowed the reporter's pen to write it on a shirt cuff.

"I'll go out first," Carpenter said. "It's better if not too many people see us together."

"I had a wife felt the same way. Uh, I need cash to get around. Them cabs is murder."

The reporter took out the envelope and counted five ten-dollar bills into Ralph's palm.

"That's it?"

He gave him another ten. "For the tip."

"You *sure* you don't work for the government?"

"My pen," Carpenter said.

"Huh? Oh." Ralph took it out of his shirt pocket.

"Keep it."

Carpenter left. Ralph was still timing his own exit when Lieutenant Bustard and a uniformed officer Ralph had never seen before came out of the men's room with their guns drawn.

The plainclothesman looked gangsterish as always in his narrow-brimmed hat and a tight navy overcoat. His pinched face appeared ruddy in the red light of the Budweiser sign in the window, the natty moustache pasted on.

"Assume the position, criminal," he said. "You're under arrest for suspicion of homicide and being a general pain in the ass."

As Ralph was being frisked by the uniform, Richard said, "Sorry, man. I got a liquor license to look out for."

"Don't sweat it." Ralph allowed himself to be handcuffed by the uniform. "Sal the Hippo will be glad to hear you been skimming the Saturday night take for that little redhead from Ferndale."

"Let's go, killer," said Bustard.

"What about my rights?"

"Looks a little more pink than your left, but I'm no expert on ladies' bedroom slippers. It isn't your color."

Ralph exercised his right to remain silent.

The interrogation room was a little larger than the bathroom of Ralph's apartment and contained a yellow oak library table with one short leg and three mismatched chairs. Ralph sat on one, rubbing his freshly unmanacled wrists and watching the clumsiest spider he had ever seen trying to spin a web in a corner of the ceiling. It kept falling off.

He had been sitting there ten minutes when Lieutenant Bustard came in. Bustard didn't have his hat on, exposing a pale bald head whose dark fringe of hair ended precisely where the hat had begun. He looked smaller without it, a bonsai cop on the bottom lip of the minimum height requirement. Ralph watched him take off his blue pinstripe suitcoat and arrange it carefully over the back of one of the vacant chairs. Everything the lieutenant wore was built to scale, from his eyelash-width moustache to his small tight vest to the delicate-looking revolver in his belt holster with its mother-of-pearl grip. When he was through smoothing the seams on the suitcoat, he drew a slim cassette tape recorder from a pocket of his vest and put it in the center of the table without turning it on.

"Comfortable?" he asked pleasantly; or as pleasantly as he could manage considering that his voice reminded dog-shy Ralph of a terrier's yap.

"My shorts are riding high. Thanks for asking."

Bustard fashioned a smile, small and pinched. "Not as tight as the fix you're in, I bet."

Ralph said nothing. He couldn't take his eyes off the uncoordinated spider. It was wobbling on the edge of its web, directly above Bustard's naked scalp.

"Who was the man you were talking to in the bar?" asked the lieutenant.

"My Mary Kay lady."

"You got a smart mouth for a dumb guy, Poteet."

"It's the shorts." It felt like he had a rock stuffed up there.

"They'll fix that in Jackson. They give you those sturdy cotton skivvies to go with the denims. Have you ever been inside? Prison, not just jail."

"My mother used to take me to visit her brother in Joliet."

"What was he in for?"

"He fell in love with a cop."

Bustard stroked both sides of his moustache. Above his head the spider was hanging on by one leg, waving the others frantically for balance. "Well, you're going to get a taste of what it's like from the wrong side of the bars. You were the last person seen with your landlord just before he disappeared."

Ralph felt some small relief. They hadn't guessed Vinnie was dead at the time. "That don't prove nothing."

"We tossed your place. The boys in the lab found some fibers imbedded in Vinnie's neck. We matched them to a tie we found hanging in your closet."

"Vinnie was always borrowing my stuff, sometimes when I wasn't home. They could of been from before."

"Normally, a man doesn't tie a tie around his bare throat."

"Who said Vinnie was normal?"

Bustard shifted gears. "You sticking to that story about your gun getting stolen before Bishop Steelcase was killed with it?"

"Yeah." Ralph was watching the spider.

Just as it lost its hold on the web, the lieutenant bent forward and turned on the tape recorder. The spider landed on the curve of his shoulder, skidded, and fell to the floor.

The recorder's speaker had a tinny sound, but Ralph recognized his own voice.

"*I'm* here, Your Bishopness," he heard himself say. "Where the fuck are you? This is gonna cost you."

Ralph said, "Who's that?"

"We wondered why there wasn't a tape in Steelcase's answering machine," Bustard said. "Then it came to police headquarters in yesterday's mail."

"You saying that's me?"

"We know you were at the rectory; you gave your card to the altar boy. You had business with the bishop, but he didn't show up, so you went to his house and shot him to death. Thanks for putting your threat on tape, Poteet. Not many killers oblige."

"That wasn't no threat!"

"What was it, a telephone solicitation?"

"It was the killer sent it! When I went to call back and leave my name, somebody hung up the phone on his end. The killer was there then. He copped the tape and sent it to you to pin the kill on me."

"You called back to leave your *name*?"

"Hey, who knew?"

Bustard tugged down the points of his vest. "The tape was mailed from the post office on Fort; dropped through the slot. We're running prints, but they'll belong to the clerks who handled the envelope. No return address, naturally. Who needs one? A voice print will prove you left the message."

"You don't even know when I left it."

"Sure I do. You just told me."

"He's gotta get rid of me. He could kill me like the others, but it's a lot simpler to get me sent up."

"Who is he?"

"I don't know."

"Ran out of lies finally?"

Ralph said, "Shit."

"You just named the creek you're up, Poteet." Bustard tapped the recorder. "We've traced two murder weapons and a clear threat straight back to you. You even *look* like someone who should go to jail. I'm betting you couldn't even dig up a character witness whose testimony wouldn't get the Michigan legislature to reinstate the death penalty just for you. I've been a cop twenty-seven years and I *never* worked a case as tight as this one. I'm going to have the transcripts bound and give away copies to my in-laws at Christmas."

He stopped talking. After a long silence he drew out the chair opposite Ralph, sat down, and rested his forearms on the table. The fluorescent lights threw haloes off his dome.

"Tell it," he said.

○○○○○○

"Tell what?"

"Everything. What was your business with the bishop and what did it have to do with the murder of Vinnie Capablanca and the attempted murder of Lyla Dane? It sure isn't as if you might talk yourself into a worse jam."

Ralph glanced at the spider, lying motionless on the floor where it had fallen. Well, at least it wasn't a roach. He drew a deep breath and released it slowly. "Can I have a matchstick?"

Chapter 28

A reel-to-reel tape recorder had been brought in and now occupied the spot where the pocket cassette machine had rested. Lieutenant Bustard and Sergeant O'Leary, the arson investigator, sat hunched on either side of it with their hands on the table and their chins on their hands, listening to Ralph's voice droning out of the speaker. They had had to record his statement all over again after the sergeant had inadvertently flipped a smoldering cigarette butt at the tape. The room still smelled of incinerated plastic.

Bustard switched off the machine. "What unmitigated horseshit."

"Monsignor Breame," O'Leary said. "He taught my boy to play baseball. The kid still can't hit a curve with his ass."

"We got a sleazy P.I.—no, check that, he isn't even employed, which makes him just a sleaze—who says he can implicate a dead bishop and the secretary of defense—"

"Attorney general," Ralph corrected.

"Why not the president?"

"Just indirectly."

"Christ." Bustard punched the rewind button on the recorder.

"What are you going to do with the tape?" O'Leary asked.

"Erase it. Or leave you alone with it and one of your goddamn butts long enough and save electricity. If this one gets to the commissioner I'll be swinging a stick on Cass by Halloween."

"Let's hang on to it."

"This isn't your case, Sergeant. I only called you in as a courtesy because you were in on the Dane thing."

O'Leary looked at Ralph again. "How can we get in touch with this Carpenter?"

"Beats me." Ralph placed a hand over the telephone number on his shirt cuff.

"We can at least call the *Post*," the sergeant told Bustard, "ask them if they have a Carpenter working for them."

"Only if this asshole pops for the toll."

"It'll only take a minute."

The tape finished rewinding. Bustard turned the machine off again. "Use an outside phone. IAD's poking through the bills this month."

O'Leary went out, trailing ashes.

Ralph broke the silence. "A cheeseburger would go real good about now."

"Eat the fucking matchstick," Bustard said.

The spider had returned to its web to continue spinning and stumbling.

O'Leary came back. His cheeks and squinched nose were flushed from the October cold. "They never heard of anyone named Carpenter."

"Ha!"

"He's undercover," Ralph said. "It's probably a blind."

"Tell it to the block captain, Poteet. You're going down and down for murder *uno*."

"What's my motive?"

"Maybe you're on a campaign to bump off everybody who's better than you. We'll tell the jury we saved the human race."

"Woman I spoke to had the answer for me right away," O'Leary said.

"So?"

"So usually they have to check. The *Post* employs a lot of people."

"It's a slick operation. You're too accustomed to the half-ass way we handle things here."

"Hey, you got me."

Bustard leered at Ralph. "That was about as tough as catching a dose of clap in a whorehouse. I knew if we staked out your favorite watering holes long enough you'd show."

O'Leary said, "Maybe everyone at the paper has instructions to deny the existence of certain reporters. You know, in case someone gets suspicious and checks up."

"You been watching *Lou Grant* reruns again. Get somebody to run this scroat down to County. I want to have the room sprayed."

"Let's put a wire on him, see what he attracts."

" 'Let's put a wire on him.' " The lieutenant sounded nastier than usual. "You got shares in Radio Shack? Take a look at the son of a bitch. He'd hock the wire on his way to Tierra del Fuego."

"Says you," Ralph said. "I don't even know where that is."

"Where's he going to run with a tail?"

Bustard was silent. Ralph thought the lieutenant was unwilling to cast doubt upon his department's surveillance with a suspect in the room. "Suppose we do put a wire on him," he said finally. "Who's he going to talk to?"

"Poteet?"

"I was thinking of giving Willard Newton a whirl." What the hell; he couldn't shake anybody down from inside the Wayne County Jail.

"Sure," said Bustard. "I bet he hops on the next plane. Who could resist an interview with a pile of human compost like you?"

"Maybe he'll send an aide."

"Kissinger, I bet."

O'Leary lit a cigarette and tossed the match over his shoulder. It burned a fresh hole in the linoleum. "We're talking cover-up and murder, Lieutenant. Newton doesn't know how much Poteet knows or that the press has found out as much as it has. At the very least he might draw fire."

"Maybe if we get real lucky Poteet will get whacked and we arrest the shooter." Bustard played with his moustache. "You're very persuasive, Sergeant."

"Do we get the wire?"

Someone knocked on the door and leaned inside. It was the uniform who had helped bring Ralph in. "Visitor here for the suspect, Lieutenant."

"His lawyer?"

"A woman."

"About eighteen, nice ass?" Ralph asked.

"That's her. Said her name's April something."

"The Dane woman's sister," O'Leary told Bustard. "That who you used your one phone call on, Poteet?"

"Everybody else I know hung up on me."

"Why didn't you tell her to wait?" Bustard demanded.

"Did I say she has a nice ass?" asked the uniform.

"Stall her. Then find Connors and tell him to bring his kit here."

"Yes sir." The uniform withdrew.

O'Leary said, "We going to do it?"

"Yeah. Maybe Connors will screw up and electrocute the bastard."

Chapter 29

*C*onnors was a rodent-faced plainclothesman with a lop-sided crewcut and slender hands like those of a concert pianist or the man who made pizzas in the window of an Italian diner. With them he opened the black vinyl case he had brought and removed a transmitter in a gray plastic shell the size of a package of cigarettes. "Strip to the waist, please."

Ralph peeled off his shirt.

"That reminds me," Lieutenant Bustard said. "I promised my wife I'd pick up some whitefish on the way home."

Connors clipped a small battery pack to Ralph's belt, plugged in the transmitter, and used adhesive tape to fix it to his chest.

"Watch the hair," said Ralph.

"What hair?"

"How come I got to wear this rig now? I ain't even made the call yet."

Bustard said, "When you aren't used to wearing one it takes some adjusting. In a day or two you'll stop stumping around like Frankenstein and nobody'll guess you're wired."

Ralph put on his shirt. "Do I turn anything on?"

"No." Connors was emphatic. "Avoid bending over, and whatever you do, don't touch it. If you change shirts, make it anything but nylon. That static electricity is murder."

"Can I fart?"

"Quietly. And try not to sweat too much. We had one short out once and catch fire."

"How *is* Appleby?" O'Leary asked.

"I ran into him the other day at K mart," Connors said. "He goes in for his last skin graft next week."

"What's it been, two years?"

"Nearer three. The guy he busted got out in July."

Ralph started unbuttoning his shirt. "I changed my mind. Put me in jail."

Bustard said, "Too late. You'll be followed by a department van with Sergeant O'Leary and Officer Connors inside. Same principle: when you get used to pulling a shadow you'll stop looking over your shoulder. What kind of car does your girlfriend drive?"

"Blue '63 Corvair. Where's my Riviera?"

"In lockup. You can pick it up at eight when the garage opens." The lieutenant regarded him. "You look like a guy who's been getting it pretty regular lately. You better do it with your pants and shirt on till we get something on tape we can use."

"Better yet, don't do it at all," said Connors. "Unless you like barbecues in bed."

"Thank you," Ralph said.

Snapping shut his case, Connors shook his head. "First time anyone ever thanked me for that."

"Your hunch better work," Bustard told O'Leary. "If I wind up back in blue I'll see they put you on park detail."

The arson investigator, banished with a fresh cigarette to the corner farthest from the delicate electronics work, ran a hand over his face, smearing it with ashes. "One killer more or less won't do much to the stats. Anyway, I sort of want to help Poteet out. He reminds me of me on the worst day I ever had."

Ralph said nothing. He had already started to sweat, and hoped the slight burning smell he detected belonged to O'Leary.

April was waiting in the squad room when he came out behind Connors. She had on the bright orange blouse she had been wearing when they met, tucked into a pleated navy skirt with a slit that showed one thigh as she walked up to him. Her black hair fell unfettered to her waist and her color was high, as if she had come there straight from bed. Not much work was getting done in the room with her in it, Ralph noticed with a surge of pride.

"Hi," she said. "You all right?"

"I'm okay. Sorry I woke you up."

"I've been spending a lot of time in bed lately, anyway. Brought you something." She held out a brightly colored plastic bag.

Ralph took it and opened it. It contained a pair of shiny black oxfords.

"I stopped in at an all-night convenience store," she said. "I hope I guessed the size right. You don't mind vinyl, do you?"

"My feet wouldn't feel right in nothing else." Sitting down carefully in a vacant desk chair, he took off the pink slippers and put on the shoes.

"Let me." She knelt to tie them. The detectives in the room directed their attention elsewhere. "There."

He wiggled his toes. They felt a little cramped, but then he had had to break in every pair of shoes he had ever owned except those he had inherited in jail. "I think I ruined your slippers," he said.

"I wrote them off when I gave them to you. Are you free to go?"

Ralph looked up at Bustard, who nodded. He stood and the

two started out. O'Leary and Connors had already gone for the van.

"You sure you're all right? You're walking a little stiff."

"Back's a little sore."

"I'll give you a rubdown when we get back to the apartment."

"No! Uh, I mean, it'll pop back. It always does. I got it 'cause of Vietnam."

"I didn't know you were in Vietnam."

"It's how I stayed out."

"You poor man." She snaked an arm around his waist. As the squad room door swung shut behind them, Ralph heard a detective say, "Maybe he cooks."

In the Corvair, Ralph turned around to look for the van. There were several parked in the Authorized Vehicles Only section; it was still dark out and he couldn't tell if any of them was occupied.

"What happened?" April started the engine.

"I walked into a net. Stupid."

"Why'd they let you go?"

He turned back to look at her. "Ain't you glad to see me?"

She smiled and patted his thigh. He willed himself to think of the plot of a Stephen King movie to bring down his instant erection. Finally she withdrew the hand to back the car out of its space. "They were looking for you for murder. How'd you convince them you're innocent?"

"I got one of them faces."

"No, really."

"They found a better suspect." He had been cautioned against mentioning the wire to anyone.

"Then you're cleared? Oh, Ralph, that's wonderful! We'll celebrate." She pulled out onto Beaubien, deserted at that young hour. Ralph saw a pair of headlights spring to life behind them and relaxed.

"If it's all the same to you, I'd rather just sack out." He

tilted his hat over his eyes. The rickety little car had a somnolent effect upon him for some reason. He suspected it had something to do with his getting away from police custody every time he rode in it.

"What you need is a long hot bath."

"Sounds good."

"With me."

Christine, he thought furiously. *Cujo. The Shining.* Jack Nicholson naked. . . .

"I bought some bubble bath at the convenience store. Somehow I knew it would come in handy. It's my only luxury. After exams I just like to stretch out my naked body in those slippery suds for hours."

Creepshow. Jesus, O'Leary and Connors were getting an earful.

"Do they know who hurt my sister?"

His erection withered. "Not yet, but they know why. What's she told you?"

"Told me? Oh. I haven't had the chance to go back and visit. I'm studying for midterms."

Pretending greater exhaustion than he felt, he drew himself up on his side in the seat, sneaking a glance through the back window. The headlights were hanging back two blocks. "So how is she? I guess you been calling the nurses' station."

"Of course. They say she's going to be all right. More reason to celebrate." Reaching for the gearshift knob, she missed and stroked Ralph's groin.

Carrie. He hadn't realized how many King titles began with C. He changed positions again, drawing the family jewels out of her reach. He was starting to feel warm in the vicinity of the transmitter; he hoped it was biological. "The cops should know how good she's doing, increase the guard," he said. "If word gets out, the guy might make another try. They can't afford no talky hookers."

"They? You mean the police?"

"No." He clamped his mouth shut. He was getting plenty talkative himself. He must have been almost as tired as he let on.

The Corvair's tires sang as they picked up speed. They had entered the northbound John Lodge. "Ralph?"

"*Salem's Lot*. I mean, yeah?"

"How much do you know about what happened to Lyla?"

"Nothing. Cops are worse than doctors when it comes to telling us joes diddly."

"Are you sure? I hired you to find out."

"Asking questions is what got me into the fix I'm in. Was in. Anyway, you can see why I don't want to collect my fee again right away. I ain't earned it."

"Oh, it wouldn't be payment. You underestimate yourself, Ralph. You're a good lover. Not at all like those boys at school."

"Oh yeah?"

"Yeah. Who needs marathon men? Afterwards I just want to go to sleep. I get plenty of rest with you."

"Oh. Yeah."

"Do you think I'm in love?"

"With your mattress."

The freeway had been resurfaced recently; the smooth ride lulled Ralph into a doze. He dreamed of clerical corpses and fiery death and strangling death and death by gunshot and heart failure and killers who turned out to be just newshawks looking for copy. He missed the old days—just last week—of erotic dreams and celibate days, even if the celibacy wasn't his idea. It was a piss-poor life, but at least it was his own, or had been.

He awoke with April unbuttoning his shirt.

". . . Just float away on all those pretty bubbles," she was saying. Her fingers found the adhesive tape. "Ralph, are you hurt?"

"No. I mean yeah. Just a cut." He slid back, but her hand pursued him. She kept her eyes on the road. Suddenly she jerked the hand away.

"That's a microphone!"

Her voice had changed. Ralph couldn't identify the change but put it down to shock. He sat up in the seat, tipping his hat back. "You want to know who tried to do Lyla, right? Well, I'm helping the cops. I'm an undercover volunteer."

Without looking away from the windshield, she reached out again, tore the transmitter's wires free of the battery pack on his belt, and threw it into the backseat, along with the adhesive and all six of the hairs on Ralph's chest.

"You could of asked me to take it off," he said, massaging the bare spot. He glanced back over his shoulder.

"Don't bother looking for your cop friends," she said. "I lost them five minutes ago."

Her tone was definitely different. It sounded harsher, deeper; not at all like that of a schoolgirl. Ralph realized then that they had left the freeway and were hurtling through a neighborhood he didn't recognize. There was not another set of headlights to be seen for blocks.

"You ain't Lyla's sister," he said then.

"Not now. Not ever."

She produced a nickel-plated revolver from the pocket on the driver's door. The sky had begun to go pale, casting a deathly shade of gray over her features. The skin was drawn tight, the skull obvious beneath. Looking from her face to the gun and back again, Ralph couldn't believe he had ever thought her to be eighteen.

Chapter 30

"*I* came up with the April Dane cover before I left Washington," she said. "The real sister is in the Washtenaw County Morgue, still awaiting identification. I was fixed to take Lyla out even before she lost her nerve."

"What about Vinnie and the bishop?"

"Your asshole landlord let himself into your apartment while I was searching for the pictures. Would you believe the little bastard tried to cut himself in on the action?"

"In a minute. Why'd you use my necktie?"

"It was handy. Also it looked like a good idea at the time. The more pressure you had on you from both sides, the easier you'd be to deal with when the time came."

"So why didn't you? Why the slap-and-tickle?"

"I had to find out where you hid the pictures you told Steelcase about, also how much you knew and who you'd told."

"Yeah?"

"You don't know shit, pal."

"I sure don't," he said, relieved. "What about the bishop?"

"He got scared and blew his own sweet setup. In return for

his cooperation with the Justice Department, he was primed for a federal appointment in Washington—church/state liaison or something on that order—but when Breame bellied up dead under the circumstances we'd arranged and you started shaking him down, he panicked. I saw that coming, too, and took him out."

"With my gun."

"I knew it'd come in handy when I found it at your place." She spun the car around a corner one-handed. The gun remained steady. "With you set to go down for two murders, I was going to let you live. Once I had the pictures."

"Sounds like a swell idea."

"That wire changes everything."

"Hey, it wasn't my idea."

"It means you found something out, or else you guessed. Now I'll have to throw you on the pile."

"If you do, the pictures go straight to the cops."

She laughed, not a pleasant sound. "What'll it tell them? Monsignor Breame got himself fucked to death. You took pictures, fell out with the hooker, burned her, tried to shake down the bishop but couldn't and killed him. Of course you would've been partners with the landlord of the building where the monsignor died, but you can't get along with anyone, it seems, and so you strangled him."

"What'd I do then, shoot myself?"

"Why not? Your blackmail scheme went south and the cops were closing in. You were facing the probability of three consecutive life sentences. Who wouldn't shoot himself?"

"You forgot Carpenter."

"Carpenter, who's Carpenter?" She looked genuinely puzzled. "You mean Steelcase's errand boy?"

"I mean the reporter for the *Washington Post*. Who do you think told me about Willard Newton?"

"You know about Newton?"

"*Everybody* knows." He pressed it. "You better just let me

go and run back to Washington, get a job with the Pentagon. They'll never find you there. We didn't even have this conversation. You can let me off up at the corner." He put a hand on his door handle.

She drew back the hammer on the revolver. "Where's Carpenter?"

"Why?"

She fired. Ralph screamed. The seat had exploded between his thighs. He read the telephone number aloud off his shirt cuff.

"It for you, peeper," April snarled. "Carpenter's next." She aimed at his chest.

He lunged for the steering wheel. The gun went off. He felt a searing pain over his left ear and his hat was plucked off his head. He was sure it was his scalp. Tires shrieked, the car went into a swerve. She was fighting for control of the wheel and the gun at the same time. Ralph had her wrist for a second, but his palm was sweaty and she tore it free. He lost sight of the gun.

The impact was far greater than he'd expected. The world went up in a flash of blinding light and he heard tearing and shattering and then nothing. All in all, it was like being in bed with April, he thought, just before he lost consciousness.

"Poteet?" Someone shook him.

"Don't hit me again, Pa," Ralph heard himself saying.

"Wake up, Poteet! It's Carpenter."

"Yeah? Sing 'Close to Me.' "

"Come out of there."

He felt himself being pulled and lifted, and then there was pavement beneath his feet. The first thing he saw was Carpenter's death-mask face very close to his. They had their arms on each other's shoulders.

"I ain't no kind of dancer," Ralph said, "and if I was, it sure wouldn't be with you."

"Wake up."

Ralph looked around, blinking. He was standing on a street he didn't know. There were lights on in houses on both sides and the sun was coming up green behind the Ford River Rouge plant. He was aware of a constant hissing.

"Someone was asking about you," he told Carpenter.

"Was it her?"

Ralph stared at the reporter's pointing finger for a moment, like a dog. Then his eyes followed it to where the woman he had known as April Dane lay sprawled through the sprung-open door on the driver's side of the Corvair. Her head was bleeding. Instinctively, Ralph placed a hand on his own scalp. He felt a pulpy mass over his left ear where a bullet had grazed the temple. Then he saw Carpenter's black station wagon—what was left of it—accordioned against the Corvair's buckled rear end. Steam poured hissing out of the radiator of the wagon. "You shouldn't drive with your lights off," Ralph said. "Is she dead?"

"She'll live to see parole, if she ever gets it. Are you all right?"

"I feel like shit."

"Then you're normal."

"How the hell did you find us?"

Carpenter reached across Ralph's chest and drew the ballpoint pen he had given him from Ralph's shirt pocket. "The local police ought to modernize," he said. "We've had these little transistorized wonders for years. It's an electronic homing device and a whole lot more."

He pushed the clicker. There was a tiny high-speed whine. Then he clicked it again.

". . . Your asshole landlord let himself into your apartment while I was searching for the pictures." April's voice sounded Liliputian coming from inside the barrel of the pen. Carpenter clicked it off.

"Too bad it don't write for shit," Ralph said. He heard sirens then.

Chapter 31

*Y*es, call him Ralph.

Not before five o'clock, though, after a tough night and tougher morning and afternoon spent at Detroit Police Headquarters. Because if you do he's liable to answer on about the sixteenth ring and say something like:

"Whoever you are, you'd better hang up right now, or I'll find out where you live and shit in your duct work."

"Ralph, this is Lyla."

"Who the hell is Lyla?"

"Lyla Dane. I'm calling from the hospital, for chrissake. You been drinking?"

His hip lay on something hard. He fished out a bottle of Mad Dog—the nastiest thing he could find with a cap on it, for a nasty mood—and drank off the dregs. "No." He dropped it on the floor.

"Seen the paper?"

"Which one?"

"Pick one. Any paper."

He had, in fact, bought a copy of the *Detroit News* on his

way back to the apartment. It lay about him in sections. U.S. ATTORNEY GENERAL IMPLICATED IN DETROIT MURDER SPREE, read the banner on the front page. A sidebar in the second section was headed, LOCAL INVESTIGATOR HELPED UNCOVER PLOT. It included a picture from an early P.I. license, a particularly hideous one that made his bad eye look like a bottle cap.

"I seen it," he said.

"Cops want my statement."

"You going to give it to them?"

"It should keep me out of the joint."

"I been wondering about that. How'd you get the monsignor upstairs? It took two of us to carry him down and we could of used two more."

"He walked up."

"He was *alive?*" Ralph sat up and propped his pillow behind his back.

"He was with a hooker. Well, she told me she was a hooker; I don't know what she told him. The woman in the paper sounds like her."

"April?" Her real name, as the police had learned from an FBI circular, was Cora Diedhoffer, age thirty, wanted in connection with a series of car bombings during a steelworkers' strike in Gary in 1981. Her live-in boyfriend, a suspected former mob button with a rap sheet going back to Nixon, was serving a life sentence in the Indiana State Penitentiary for one of the bombings, in which a man had been killed.

"I'm pretty sure," Lyla said. "She's the one set it up with me, said she was going to talk him into coming to try and talk me out of the life, then drug him and put him in my bed. We was going to take pictures and blackmail him after. Only he died."

"She didn't kill him?"

"I don't think so. It looked like a real heart attack to me. We put him in my bed—that was as hard a job of work I done since I took on the Anderson quintuplets—and she told me to call the cops. They wouldn't investigate too hard, she said; the Church'd see to that. Then she left and I called you. I got to work in this town."

"She came back," Ralph said. "She's the one rigged your place."

"I guessed that. It's why I didn't say nothing."

After a little silence Ralph said, "Sorry about your sister."

"I haven't seen her since I left home. We were strangers." She paused. "I just wanted to call and say thanks."

"You're gonna have to speak up. I'm a little deaf in one ear since this morning. I thought you said thanks."

"That's what I said."

He paused. "I don't think nobody ever thanked me for nothing before. Well, except April, and that didn't turn out so good."

"Well, somebody has now. I don't know when I'll see you. They want to hang on to me here for another week, and then I don't know what the cops will want. I thought I better say it now."

"Okay."

They hung up.

The telephone rang ten minutes later.

"Whoever you are, you're dead," Ralph said.

"Ralph, this is Neal."

"Then you're a dead Neal. I only got to bed at three. It's five-fifteen!"

"Thanks. You seen the papers?"

"Yeah." This time he didn't ask which one.

"Funny, I didn't see nothing in it about my cut."

"I was going to call you about that."

"And say what?"

Ralph blew a loud raspberry into the mouthpiece and pegged the receiver. Then he picked it up again and left it off the hook.

ooooo

He must have replaced it in his sleep, however, because an hour later it rang again.

"AIDS Hotline," he grumbled.

"Poteet?"

It was a woman's voice.

"Depends on who's asking."

"This is Lucille Lovechild. Have you seen the papers?"

"All of 'em."

"That was quite an investigation you pulled off. I suppose some kind of congratulations are in order."

"Hurts, don't it?" He raised himself again. This was almost worth getting stiffed by Carpenter; the reporter seemed to think that saving Ralph's life wiped out the sixteen hundred dollars he owed Ralph. "I guess you called to offer me my old job back. Well, I should make you squirm, but I won't. I need a raise, though, hunnert bucks a month. And an office with a window."

"You do have a sense of humor, Neanderthal though it is. I can appreciate it now that you're no longer working here."

"No openings, huh."

"As it happens there is one, although I'd sooner hire the Ayatollah. I fired Chuck Waverly this morning."

"How come?"

"He came staggering in two hours late, howling drunk and screaming something about turtles. I couldn't make any sense of it."

"Victorian turtles?"

"Something like that. Does it mean anything to you?"

"Are you wearing that lace-necked blouse of yours today?"

She paused. "I am, as a matter of fact. Why?"

"Nothing. My mind wandered."

"You shouldn't. It's not big enough to cross the street alone."

"Hey, I don't need to get called stupid in my own place. I can go anywhere for that."

"I'm sure," she said. "The reason I called, when you left here you took the key to the file room with you. I want it back."

"When your twat thaws out, Lucy." He cut the connection with a bang.

He stayed awake for a while after that, staring at the instrument. When it rang next time, however, he had gone back to sleep sitting up.

"Hell-o," he said musically.

"Mr. Poteet?"

Another woman.

"At your kind service."

"This is Grace Capablanca. Vincenzo's widow?"

"Whatever can I do for you, Mrs. C.?"

"I'm calling all the tenants to let them know I'm flying out next week to take over management of the building. I've decided to turn it into condominiums. You will have thirty days to come up with two hundred thousand dollars to buy your apartment or move out. Have a nice day."

Ralph wished her the same and replaced the handset gently.

Some days it just didn't pay to answer the telephone.

Bantam is proud to announce the publication of
Loren D. Estleman's newest novel,

WHISKEY RIVER

Set in Prohibition-era Detroit, this long-awaited
tale of crime and punishment is the opening blast
in a three-volume fusillade of fiction that will chron-
icle life in the Motor City (Estleman's town) in this
most violent century.

From the acclaimed author of the Amos Walker
mysteries, of *Peeper* and *Bloody Season*, here
is a novel sure to delight Estleman's faithful fans
and to win him new admirers.

Welcome to the Black Bottom

We have the biggest of nearly everthing: the tallest
building, the biggest electric sign, the longest bridge,
the most money . . .
>   —*Detroit City Directory,*
>   1925–26 edition

The "blind pig" conditions are worse in every way
than in any other town I visited, and the liquor sold
is of a ruinous quality.
>   —Ernest W. Mandeville,
>   "Detroit Sets a Bad Example,"
>   *Outlook,* April 1925

I saw Jack Dance the first time in Hattie Long's place on Vernor the night the bulls tipped it over. I guess he was going by John Danzig at the time.

Hattie hadn't been renting the place long. I remember my hack and I drove up and down the East Side for almost an hour looking for the stuffed rooster in the window. The rooster went everywhere Hattie went and it was how you could tell where she was set up on any particular night. For all the bulls cared most of the time, she could have advertised in the *Free Press*, but Hattie always had a keener sense of the proprieties than any of the auto-money hags in Grosse Pointe. Last I heard she was running a beergarden in Royal Oak or somewhere. I heard she lost her looks.

The rooster this time was in a window on the ground floor of a house with an undertaker's sign out front. She sublet it to the digger during the day and stored the liquor in coffins in back. The joke that made the rounds ran that you could get a bier in the daytime and a beer at night.

I sent the hack on his way and went in through the front. Although the side door was customary in those places, this one was five feet wide and meant for carrying out the stiffs, and not many cared to use it. We were superstitious in those days.

Hattie had about an hour between the time the mortuary closed and she opened for the night, but you'd have thought she had a week. The burgundy velvet curtain that separated the entryway from the slumber room had been pushed back, tables and chairs set in place, and a cherrywood bar with a brass footrail erected on the platform where in all probability a corpse had lain in state that afternoon. In place of the stand where visitors signed in stood two antique slot machines weighing two hundred pounds apiece. The bartender, whose name was Johnston, had on a white apron and a red bow tie on a shirt with garters. He parted his hair in the middle and waxed his handlebars like in pre-Prohibition days, but there wasn't anything affected about it because he'd been mixing drinks for forty years; his favorite boast was that he had once served a pink gin to Bat Masterson. Nobody ever called him on it, not with a faded sepia photograph of a young Johnston sparring with Jim Jeffries tacked to the wall behind the bar. The place smelled of needle beer and Lifebuoy soap from the cribs on the second floor and "Ramona" was playing on a wind-up Victrola by the big door. Hattie hated jazz.

This kid—I guessed he was twenty, but it turned out later he was barely eighteen—was leaning on the bar with his back to me, watching something. I noticed him because of his size and because the pants of the brown suit he had on were swinging a good three inches shy of his big wingtips. He was built like a lug and if I hadn't seen his face a minute later I'd have thought he was older still.

"How's the boy, Johnnie?" I asked Johnston, clearing a space for my elbows next to the kid. The bars were always crowded in places where there was no one to wait tables, with two full glasses in front of each beer drinker in case the kegs ran out.

"What'll it be?" Johnston wasn't much for the small talk.

I skidded a half-dollar across the bar and told him the usual. He poured two fingers of Old Log Cabin into a tumbler half full of Vernor's— Vernor's on Vernor, that's how I remember where the blind pig was.

The kid had turned around and looked at me when I said "Johnnie"—they were still calling him John then as I said—and that's when I found out he was a kid. He had some baby fat, and curly black hair that needed cutting. It would still need cutting years later when he had a Duesenberg and a tailor to make sure his cuffs came to his shoes. That night he looked like one of the big Polish line workers from Hamtramck that got tired of buying their boilermakers from a parked car in front of Dodge Main and came downtown. They were all youngsters.

He lost interest in me when he figured out I wasn't addressing him and returned his attention to the other end of the bar, where a shrimp in a cloth cap and a green tweed suit too heavy for the weather stood fishing in his pants pockets. He came up with a quarter and put it on the bar. Johnston filled a schooner with beer from the keg and set it down directly on top of the quarter. The shrimp put a hand on his cap, tipped down the beer in one easy installment, belched dramatically, set down the empty schooner, and put the coin back in his pocket. Then he went out past the velvet curtain. He was weaving a little.

"Who is that guy?" the kid asked Johnston.

"What guy?" The bartender swept the glass off the bar and plunged it into a washtub full of soapy water at his feet.

"The little guy. I been watching him for an hour. Every time he comes back from the toilet he slaps a two-bit piece on the bar, you draw him a beer, he drinks it and puts away his money. I seen him drink six beers and you never took the two-bit piece once. Who's he, the mayor?"

"Jerry the Lobo." Johnston shook the suds off the schooner and wiped it dry with his towel.

"Lobo like in wolf? He looks more like a rat. I seen him try to pick a guy's pocket. He got his hand slapped."

"Not lobo like in wolf," I said. "Lobo like in lobotomy."

The kid looked at me with more interest this time. I tapped my forehead. "Croakers in Jackson cut a piece out of his brain. He was a first-class pickpocket when they sent him up the last time. They did it to relieve him of his criminous intentions. Didn't work. He's still a pickpocket; he's just not too good at it anymore."

"Bullshit."

"You can see the scar when he takes the cap off."

"They *do* that?"

"Only if you volunteer. They knocked time off his sentence for it. Anyway, that's why no bartender I know will take his quarter. They feel sorry for him."

"It's always the same quarter?"

"Far as I know."

"Hell, I'd do better than that. If I had a gun I'd put him out of his misery."

I never forgot that, what Jack Dance said about putting Jerry the Lobo out of his misery. Maybe I would have, except that time in Hattie's was the last time I saw Jerry. He disappeared soon after.

The kid stuck out a right hand the size of a bucket. "I'm John Danzig."

"Jew?"

"What if I am?" He drew back the hand.

"Don't get your balls in an uproar, junior. I'm Greek myself." I offered him mine. "Connie Minor."

"Connie?"

"Short for Constantine. Some civil jerk at Ellis Island changed the old man's name from Minos."

He took my hand then. His was softer than I'd expected. He wasn't using it to pull any levers at the Dodge plant. For all that I felt a crackle when we made contact. It was like petting a cat on a dry winter day. "You work here, Connie?"

"Just on this highball. I write for the *Times*."

"No kidding? Who owns this joint, Connie?"

"You thinking of buying it?" I was sore about the way he'd dismissed my profession with two words. Most people were curious about it. Radio was boring as hell then and people got most of their entertainment from movies and the tabloids.

"I'm looking for a job," he said.

"What do you do?"

"Right now I help out my old man in his shop. He repairs watches. My fingers are too big, though. Also I like to see. My old man's eyes started to go when he was thirty. He's almost blind, my old man."

I wanted to laugh. If he'd ever called his father "my old man" before that night, he'd probably gotten slapped silly. Except for his size he made me think of a squirt trying to talk his way in with the big kids.

"Well, you came to the right place," I said. "They don't fix watches here."

"Fresh transfusion, sport?" Johnston asked the kid.

He put a hand around his half-empty schooner, which he'd obviously forgotten about. "One's the limit."

"We sell drinks here. We don't rent glasses."

The kid dug around inside his pockets and came up with a handful of lint. I bounced a quarter off the bar. Johnston caught it and set a full glass next to the first one.

"Thanks," said the kid. "I really do stop at one."

"Johnston doesn't care if you drink it. His mother told him if he didn't use his bar space she'd give it to the Albanians."

"You didn't say who owns the place."

"Ask Hattie."

Hattie was coming our way from the back where they dressed and painted the stiffs. She was five-two but looked taller because she was so slender, and the drop-waisted flapper dresses she wore added to the impression of height. She was a strawberry blonde, bobbed and marcelled, with a broad forehead, a chin that came to a point, and a mouth that was a little too wide for the beestung lips that Mae Murray was making famous in the movies. Her eyebrows were big surprised circles of thin pencil. The gamblers at the *Times* were betting she traced them around Mason lids, but I'd seen her draw them on with only the aid of a mirror. Hattie and I went back a few. I remember how calm she looked that night, with all hell breaking loose upstairs and about to come barreling through the front door.

I was in the middle of introducing the kid to her when she put a hand on my arm. "Connie, I need to borrow you."

I gave the kid the high sign and walked off with her a few steps. She looped her arm through mine.

"They put strychnine in my best whiskey." she said. "I've got a dead justice of the peace upstairs and an Oklahoma oilman throwing up in the toilet."

"What brand?" I'd been swilling Old Log Cabin for ten minutes.

"Stop worrying about yourself. You don't think I serve this radiator juice to the guests upstairs."

"Who did it?"

"The Purples, the Little Jewish Navy, who cares? I've got to get these slot machines out of here before the bulls come and smash them to pieces. They're worth more than what's inside them."

"Did you call Joey?"

"It'll take Joey's people twenty minutes to get here. I need muscle now."

We were standing in front of one of the machines, a baroque nightmare in worked bronze with claw feet and a lever the size of a mop handle. I put my arms around it and heaved. The back legs came up an inch. I let it fall back with a crash. The record on the Victrola skipped a beat; one less fucking boop-boop-a-doo.

"You still need muscle," I said. "I haven't lifted anything heavier than a paragraph since I left the loading dock. What's wrong with Johnston?"

"He's got a hernia older than I am."

"This is your lucky night. That big kid at the bar's looking for work."

She glanced that way. The kid was glaring at Jerry the Lobo, who had just come back from the toilet and was playing the gag with the quarter again.

"Can we trust him?"

"Honey, you can't trust me. I came here looking for a story. One poisoned j.p. in a whorehouse could get me my own column."

"How you going to write it with ten broken fingers?"

I watched her. Hattie never smiled. If she ever told a joke no one knew it. "Even Joey Machine wouldn't touch a member of the press."

"How long you know Joey?" she said. "What's the kid's name?"

"John something. He's a sheeny."

"Well, he don't look like a Purple. Let's go talk to him."

That was how Jack Dance got in with the Machine mob, although he didn't know it at the time. Joey Machine had a part interest in most of the better blind pigs and hook shops on the East Side and owned Hattie Long's establishment outright. The kid listened to as much of the tale as Hattie told and said he'd be glad to help. He was smart enough not to impose conditions. All his life Jack Dance was a creature of instinct and it never let him down until the last.

"My brother can help," he said, and added: "He's a poet."

I didn't know what that had to do with anything, but we accompanied the kid to a table where a sandy-haired sheik in his twenties was talking with one of Hattie's girls over a bottle of gin with a Canadian label and a Dearborn ancestry. His suit was a better fit than his brother's but it was strictly Hudson's basement just the same. There was no family resemblance that I could see. He was built along slighter lines and his complexion was fair. I wondered if they were just close friends who considered themselves related, like the coloreds; but the kid introduced him as Tom Danzig.

"Your brother says you're a poet," Hattie said.

He played with his glass and never drank from it all the time we were there. The two had that in common at least. "I'm trying to be a writer. John thinks everyone who writes is a poet."

Hattie said, "All we need is a strong back. I don't care if you can rhyme."

He was slower to volunteer than his brother. On that short acquaintance I could see he was the thinker of the team, measuring everything against the consequences and what it meant to him. I don't know why that irritated me. With all the things Jack did later and everything he became, I always liked him. and I never liked Tom. But then I gave up trying to figure myself out years ago.

Finally he agreed to lend a hand. Hattie told Johnston, who left the bar and trundled the big White truck they used for a moving van around to the side door, and with Hattie directing us to look out for the handles and gimcrackery the three of us carried out the slot machines. We got the truck doors closed just as the sirens came within hearing. Whoever had poisoned the whiskey had given the stuff time to take effect before placing his anonymous call to the bulls. It turned out to be just time enough for us. The Danzig brothers and I were sharing a table and a bottle inside with Hattie tending bar when Lieutenant Valery Kozlowski showed up with the walking sputum from the Detroit Prohibition Squad.

About the Author

LOREN D. ESTLEMAN, a former Detroit-area newspaperman, knows his city from the bottom up. His work ranges from mainstream fiction through westerns, criticism, and new adventures of Sherlock Holmes to mysteries that put him in "the top echelon of American private-eye specialists" (*The New York Times*). He lives with his wife in Whitmore Lake, Michigan.

Kinsey Millhone is...

"The best new private eye." *—The Detroit News*

"A tough-cookie with a soft center." *—Newsweek*

"A stand-out specimen of the new female operatives."
—Philadelphia Inquirer

Sue Grafton is...

The Shamus and Anthony Award winning creator of Kinsey Millhone and quite simply one of the hottest new mystery writers around.

BANTAM MYSTERY COLLECTION